ANYTHING YOU CAN DO

Sara Garrett

A KISMET® Romance

METEOR PUBLISHING CORPORATION
Bensalem, Pennsylvania

To Samantha for 17+ years of love.
and
To Max for believing.

SARA GARRETT

Sara Garrett has supported her writing habit by working as a legal secretary, real estate agent, legal assis-
tant, leasing agent, executive secretary, and a few
others. She looks upon those jobs as research for
her writing. A native Oklahoman (McAlester) and
naturalized Texan (Dallas), Sara now lives in Lee's
Summit, Missouri, with her husband and two dogs.
Her interests, besides writing, are chocolate and
Classic Coke.

ONE

_____ **ONE** _____

"If you're determined to push down a tree, why don't you try that one over there? The scenery's better."

Bailey Russell paused in her efforts to stretch her hamstring muscles and followed the direction of Jodi's gaze, to the tall man on the other side of the trail. Like her, he leaned forward, both arms braced against a tree, muscular legs stretched behind him. His head bent forward in concentration, hiding his face, showing only a crop of thick, razor-cut black hair.

Bailey tilted her head back and laughed into the bright blue sky. "You've been in Kansas City less than twenty-four hours, and you'll probably have a date by tonight. Some things never change. As I recall, you were the only girl in Haywood High history to have three dates for the prom."

"It was only two, and I tried to give you one."

For an instant, the memory tugged Bailey back to the painful days of being a scrawny, awkward adolescent, the butt of jokes about red hair and freckles and brainy women. But with a shake of her head, she dispelled the past, then stretched again, savoring the present, her status as a successful attorney, the no longer

7

awkward body, the smooth response of well-toned muscles.

Her gaze shifted involuntarily across the way, to the long legs stretched out behind the dark-haired man. A quick thrill shot through her at the sight, a thrill she immediately quelled. Of course, it was only a thrill of admiration, she assured herself. Impersonal admiration of good musculature. She wasn't leering at him or anything silly.

Thus reassured, she allowed her gaze to travel up his body, past the flat stomach encased in silky running shorts, over the pectorals bulging under the thin material of his T-shirt. He lacked the lean, streamlined upper body of a serious runner, would be more at home in the gym, obviously worked with weights.

Then her eyes met his impossibly blue ones, saw he was watching her and smiling. Caught! Abruptly ducking her head, she concentrated on her exercises, tried to tell herself she had no reason to be embarrassed. The man probably scarcely noticed her watching him since he was undoubtedly focusing on Jodi.

"Go get him, kiddo," she said brusquely. "You've got his attention now."

"I don't think—" Jodi began.

"I've got to go find my spot," Bailey interrupted as the man pushed away from his tree and strode toward them. Jamming her sun visor over her cropped auburn hair, she turned to leave. There was no reason for her to hang around and watch him flirt with Jodi when she'd just made a colossal fool of herself gawking at him—studying his musculature, she corrected.

She did, however, pause long enough to turn back with a grin. "But take note, the man's wearing a green T-shirt. Only we members of the Bar Association, our race sponsor, got green ones. And I do recall that you said you're allergic to lawyers." With a wave and a laugh, Bailey jogged away just as the dark-haired man came up.

When the five-minute warning buzzer sounded, Bailey watched in surprise as the man in question moved into the front ranks of the group of almost nine hundred runners. Since race etiquette dictated everyone line up according to speed, the man obviously thought he would finish in the first group. Bailey didn't think so. Not with all that weight in his chest and arms.

On a hunch, she looked down at his shoes. New— not a speck of dirt on them. Since no one could be stupid enough to come to a 10K race with shoes that hadn't been broken in, she could only assume he did his running indoors. She could imagine his surprise when he came to the first hill, a geographical feature noticeably absent from health clubs. He wouldn't be smiling so broadly then. That perfect hair might even get mussed.

The starter's gun sounded, and the crowd plunged ahead.

Bailey forced herself to settle into an easy, loping gait. She yearned to stretch her long legs to their limit, pass everyone, and run straight up into the crystal blue prairie sky, but common sense tugged on the reins. Six and two-tenths miles was a long way to run. Pacing was all-important.

She soon found her stride and began to run effortlessly. As she moved from the shade of a tree into the sunlight, then back into the shade, as the cool morning breeze stroked her cheeks, she gloried in the joy of running, almost forgot that the purpose of the race was to win. She drew in a deep breath, picturing it full of rich oxygen from the forest of trees along the path through the Corporate Woods area, felt that richness flowing through her blood, energizing her body.

"I see we're in the same profession."

The voice jarred into her concentration, causing her to make a misstep and lose her stride.

The dark-haired man ran beside her. Knowing he was a lawyer, Jodi had doubtless sent him packing, and now he thought he'd get to her through her friend. He wouldn't be the first to try *that*.

"I doubt it," she snapped. "I'm a thief. I stole this shirt from the lawyer who's defending me."

She increased her pace slightly, pulling away from him, concentrating on regaining her stride.

When the water table at the end of three miles came into view, she still had scarcely broken a sweat. Neither, she noted as she approached, had her friend, Gordon Thomas, but at least he *had* made it out of bed in time to help at the table.

She smiled as she watched her friend, perfectly tanned and immaculately clad in white shorts, lounging beside the bottled water, handing out soggy paper cups. Gordon had probably never broken a sweat in his life, except in a sauna or steam room.

"There are people ahead of you in this race!" Gordon exclaimed, holding out two paper cups. "It's not like either of you to allow that."

"I'm still running faster than you are," she retaliated. At the same time a familiar voice declared, "The race isn't over yet," and as she reached for one of the cups, another hand clasped the same one.

She looked up into electric blue eyes. At least the man wasn't smiling anymore. He looked as confused as she felt.

"I have two cups," Gordon said. "One for each of my friends."

"You know him?" Bailey asked.

"Turn loose of the cup, both of you," Gordon insisted, offering two fresh waters. "Of course I know him. This is Austin Travers. Austin, Bailey Russell."

With a brief nod of acknowledgment, Bailey accepted a new cup, gulped the tepid water, and tossed the paper into a convenient barrel. "See you at the awards, if you don't fall asleep and miss the whole thing," she called to Gordon as she loped away, consciously controlling her pace, resisting an urge to run full out until she left those strange eyes far behind.

How distressing to find that man was Austin, Gordon's old college buddy. Gordon had been anticipating Austin's impending arrival in Kansas City for some time, and she'd been looking forward to meeting him, to having another friend like the easygoing Gordon. So much for that notion.

She forced herself to concentrate on the run, on getting back into her satisfying rhythm. The race was about half over, and already her steady pace was carrying her past many of the runners who'd passed her earlier. At the end of the next mile she could begin to stretch out a little, start to move up, then sprint the final mile.

"Gordon's told me a lot about you, Bailey Russell."

Bailey almost stumbled. The man was persistent, give him that. And now that she knew who he was, she supposed she had to be nice to him.

"Ditto," she said. No point in overdoing the niceness, however.

"He and I went to school together," he continued.

"Yes," Bailey acknowledged. "So I've heard."

And now she could see the stories in a different light. Gordon, who'd been born with a platinum American Express card in his mouth, had been so proud of his self-made friend. Austin had put himself through school with jobs and scholarships while still having the best grades, the prettiest women, the most honors. She'd assumed all those things would matter as little to his friend as they did to Gordon—a likely erroneous assumption. Though to be fair, she supposed she'd have to give him the benefit of incomplete evidence thus far. Just because he looked like a movie star and appeared accustomed to having women fall at his feet didn't necessarily make him all bad.

"Gordon tells me you've come all the way over from

St. Louis to shape up Kearns, Worley's branch here in Kansas City," she said, making an effort to be polite.

"I missed the last partners' meeting and got elected." He tossed the information out casually, though it was a glaringly obvious way to work into the conversation that he was a partner. So much for incomplete evidence. The man was an arrogant jerk, no doubt about it.

Since she couldn't think of any subtle way to retaliate by letting him know that she was up for a partnership in the very near future, she just kept running, increasing her pace slightly even though they were starting up a hill.

He stayed right with her, and while his face was shiny with perspiration, he continued to breathe through his nose, a feat she was finding increasingly difficult. She grudgingly gave him credit. He was doing a lot better than she'd expected.

"That hill was a killer, wasn't it?" he asked as they started down the other side.

She smiled. She'd been right about the health club. This was probably the first hill he'd ever run. "Wait till you get to the one at the end of the fifth mile. We're talking serial killer."

"You sound like you're familiar with the route."

"I've run here a couple of times."

"I've only run sporadically since the high school track team."

Aha, Bailey thought. Already he's making excuses for losing. She increased her pace again, but again he refused to fall back.

"Twenty-eight thirty!" a voice announced.

Bailey's attention snapped to the volunteer with the stopwatch calling out the four-mile time. The marker must be short. Her time should be closer to thirty minutes. Austin didn't seem to notice, and she wasn't about to tell him. Let him relax, think he was doing better than he really was, then she'd run the socks off him.

They strode along in silence for a few minutes. He really did keep an awfully good pace for someone of his size.

"You don't look like a runner," she finally said.

"You do," he answered, and something in his voice made her glance his way, into his bright, appraising gaze.

She directed her attention back to running. That particular stare was undoubtedly calculated to make women melt—a weakness to which she was fortunately immune. Nevertheless, it was time to speed up again.

Adrenaline and endorphins gushing, running on a high, almost flying, she found herself smiling. Only from the joy of the exercise, she assured herself, not from Austin's comments. Nevertheless, she quickly erased the smile lest he see it and think she'd been taken in by his erotic eyes.

Almost without conscious effort, her pace increased a little more. By the time the two of them reached the "killer hill at the end of the fifth mile," however, Bailey thought she just might have pushed a bit too hard. She gave serious consideration to crawling up the hill.

"How you doing?" Austin asked as they began the climb. It was his first comment in quite a while, and Bailey was grateful for more than one reason. She had no energy left to talk, needed it all for running.

"Great," she answered in a breathy grunt, the most articulate sound of which she was capable. She'd die before she'd let him know how close to the end she was, before she'd expose a weakness, leaving herself vulnerable.

Her legs were numb, but that was better than pain. As long as she could persuade her brain to keep ordering them forward, they'd be okay. However, the pressure in her chest and the ache in her side were very distracting. She decided to wait until the last half mile to sprint past him.

The hill stretched longer than ever. The street department must have added an extra block or two.

Finally the finish line loomed ahead. Less than half a mile to go. Time to sprint for it, leave Austin Travers far behind with his toothpaste smile and blue contact lenses—for surely his eyes weren't really that bright. Her brain ordered her legs to stretch out farther, move faster. She thought they were following orders, but somehow Austin stayed beside her, a permanent fixture in her peripheral vision.

She pushed harder. The red FINISH banner grew larger, but the letters began to blur. Reaching deep inside, Bailey found an extra ounce of energy and stretched farther, churned her legs faster. From the corner of her eye, she saw Austin move ahead, cross the line a split second before her.

She wanted to curse, but couldn't. Breathing was an all-consuming activity. She stopped for removal and recordation of her number, then stumbled on to the end of the women's chute.

"That was *incredible*!" Jodi shouted, grabbing her arm.

Bailey wanted to protest that it wasn't incredible, that Austin had beaten her, but the words wouldn't come out. She took the cup of water Jodi offered and raised it to her lips, rinsing her mouth. Swallowing would have meant a brief cessation of breathing, and she needed all the oxygen she could get right now.

She scanned the crowd but didn't see Austin. That was good, because she was pretty sure she was going to throw up from the extreme exertion, and she had no intention of letting him know how tough the race had been. Moving shakily, she made her way to the sidelines, aware that Jodi was talking, but too intent on her body's agonies to catch the words.

As she concentrated on walking out her cool-down, ignoring her protesting muscles that wanted to rest, breathing fast enough to get adequate oxygen into her system to avoid passing out, Jodi's words suddenly penetrated.

"My time?" she gasped, not sure she'd heard right.

"Yes," Jodi assured her, "forty-two minutes, seven seconds."

Suddenly it didn't matter quite so much that Austin had beaten her, because she'd just beaten herself, turned in a personal best. As soon as she was physically able, she planned to shout to the heavens.

Jodi grabbed two oranges from a refreshment table and began peeling as they walked. "I see you came in with that gorgeous lawyer," she said, offering a half-skinned fruit to Bailey. "Do you have something to tell me?"

Bailey gulped down a piece of orange, greedy for the sugar and liquid to nourish her exhausted system. "Gordon's friend," she gasped. "Thought you weren't interested in lawyers."

"I can admire a thing of beauty while having no desire to mate with it. Anyway, he passed me by with a wave. I think he's interested in you."

Even though it sent her into coughing, gasping spasms, Bailey burst into laughter at the idea. Men like Austin Travers reserved their interest for beautiful women with soft voices and bust line measurements that exceeded their IQs.

On the other side of the path, Austin held his side to ease the stitch and walked around the sidelines, fighting the nausea of overexertion, trying to cool down slowly. Across the crowd, he caught a glimpse of the woman who'd almost killed him.

He studied her for a moment, watched her accept an orange from her friend. When he'd first seen her before the race, stretching her long, sleek muscles, she'd seemed a regal gazelle. She enhanced that image when she ran with long, graceful strides, hair sparking red in the sunlight. Now, however, he knew her to be a tiger, a force to be reckoned with.

If he could just manage to catch his breath, he'd go over and congratulate her on a race well run. Not to mention that she'd pushed him into his best time since the high school track team. But by the time he got back in control, ready to face her, she and her friend had disappeared into the crowd.

Feeling oddly disappointed and deflated, he got a cold soda and wandered through the throng.

"Austin! Over here!"

Austin turned at the welcome sound of Gordon's voice and saw him standing under a large tree, waving. Beside Gordon, Bailey and her friend lounged on the grass. Sunlight dappled Bailey's smooth, sweat-shiny skin and blazed in her hair. However, her gaze was cool and green as she watched him approach.

The combination of fire and ice was daunting and tantalizing. He'd probably be wise to keep on running. Instead he sank to the ground beside her.

"Bailey's trying to make me take up some exhausting sport," Gordon complained as Austin sank to the cool grass, "and Jodi Duvall, whom you haven't met and probably don't want to, thinks I should find a decent job."

"Make something of yourself," Jodi supplied, laughing, looking up at Gordon. "Better yourself. Become a janitor, wash dishes, dig ditches."

"But Bailey's a lawyer, and you like her," Gordon objected.

Jodi sighed heavily, lowering her eyes in mock shame. "I'm partially to blame for her sorry lot in life. From the time we were in third grade, I encouraged her to go to law school. I blame it all on too many Perry Mason reruns."

"What is this?" Austin asked, laughing. "Are we trashing attorneys?"

"Why not?" Jodi quipped. "Can you think of anybody who deserves it more?"

"I asked her to marry me," Gordon declared, leaning lazily back against the tree trunk. "She told Bailey I showed good sense in not running or indulging in those other activities that make you sweat, so naturally I asked her to marry me. That's when she said I'd have to get a decent job."

The sound of Bailey's throaty laughter drew Austin's attention to her. She was leaning back on her arms, long legs stretched in front of her, the corners of her full mouth tilted upward, once again the sleek, sensuous woman he'd noticed earlier rather than the tiger he'd almost lost the race to.

But then she turned toward him, eyes narrowing, smile challenging. "Jump in, Austin," she dared him, sitting upright, pulling her knees to her chest and leaning her chin on them. "Defend your chosen profession."

Austin cleared his throat, suddenly at a loss for words, inexplicably feeling eighteen years old again, with the task of proving himself still looming ahead. "What exactly don't you like about lawyers?" he asked, seeking the contrast of Jodi's easy, laughing features that belied her barbed words.

"I've been a legal secretary for twelve years. Need I say more?"

"I promise not to hold that against you if you don't hold my law degree against me," he retorted with a smile.

"I'll try, counselor, but these ingrained prejudices are hard to overcome. Are you with the same firm as these two?"

"No," he said. "Does that make it better or worse?"

"A little better, I suppose. Gives you some distance, at least. You see, I go back home to Haywood tomorrow to pack my bags, move in with Bailey next Saturday, and go to work for Hoskins, Grier and Morris on Monday. Since secretaries and lawyers are natural enemies, there's absolutely no chance for Gordon and me to be friends." She sighed in exaggerated fashion.

"Unfortunate, really. He has some good qualities, like being rich, lazy, and blond, but hey, that's life."

Austin laughed in genuine delight. Jodi was witty, entertaining, and attractive. A quick glance at Gordon convinced him he shouldn't go any further than admiring her, though. He'd known Gordon a long time, but he'd never seen him look at a woman like that—kind of a combination of the ways he used to look at his dog and the *Playboy* centerfold.

Well, if she and Gordon developed a relationship, at least the three of them could get along. However, he wasn't too sure about Bailey. How was it possible with only a glance she could make him feel the way he'd felt those early years in school and in his law practice—like he had to work twice as hard just to catch up with the rest of the world?

From the corner of his eye, he watched her stretch her long legs across the grass.

She made him feel frustrated, defensive, and, damn it, exhilarated in anticipation of the challenge, an aspect of those early years he'd forgotten until now.

The waitress left with their post-race breakfast order. Jodi disappeared behind a small newspaper she'd picked up as they came into the coffee shop while Austin and Gordon discussed the fate of a mutual friend from college days. Bailey settled back in the plastic-covered booth, sipped her soda, and thought again of the awards ceremony.

She still couldn't decide if she should be proud of winning a second-place medal in her age and sex division. Ordinarily second place, especially with the age and sex qualifiers, was the same as losing. Still, Austin didn't get a medal even though he'd beaten her. So that kind of meant he hadn't really beaten her . . . didn't it?

And he had run one hell of a race, hadn't held back just because she was a woman. Besting him would be a noteworthy accomplishment—and a far safer one than getting pulled under by those vibrant eyes so full of energy and life, those thighs with the well-defined muscles that looked as if they'd be rock-hard to the touch. Not, of course, that she was in any danger of that.

"Hey, listen to this!" Jodi smoothed her newspaper onto the table. " 'SWM, thirty-two, professional, seeks long-term relationship with attractive, single woman, twenty-six to thirty-five.' Could this be the father of my future children? Nope, he smokes."

"What on earth have you got there?" Bailey demanded, glad to have a new direction for her wayward thoughts.

"*The Kansas City Observer*. It has this section called 'New Friends.' There's pages and pages of ads. I've heard that's the 'in' way to meet people now."

"I wouldn't think you'd have any trouble finding dates," Austin assured her.

The man really was dense. Bailey didn't see how Jodi could have made it any clearer that she didn't want to date an attorney, but he kept trying.

"I'm not looking for 'dates,' " Jodi advised him. "I could have stayed in Haywood if all I'd wanted was dates with male bodies. I'm looking for a relationship with someone who's intelligent, romantic, exciting, funny, handsome . . . Hmm . . . 'Degreed DWM, professional, divorced two years, no diseases . . .' Oh, gag."

"Prince Charming," Gordon contributed. "She's looking for Prince Charming, but no lawyers need apply."

"That's a great idea," Jodi said, folding the paper. "I'll run my own ad. 'Looking for Prince Charming, no lawyers need apply,' although the exclusion should be self-evident."

"Ah, revenge will be sweet," Gordon drawled, raising his eyes to the ceiling. "Stafford Morris, for all those weekends you made me work and all the nasty memos, not to mention the cigar smoke, behold your secretary.''

"May the two of them have a long, long relationship." Bailey lifted her soda in a mock toast. "Our beloved managing partner," she explained to Austin.

"I've met the man," he acknowledged, and Bailey wanted to ask the circumstances, why his lips thinned when he made the curt remark. But before she could decide on a polite way to frame her question, the food arrived, and conversation ceased.

Stuffed and exhausted, Bailey pushed open the door of her second-floor condominium and stooped to catch the tiny bundle of black and red fur that launched itself into her arms.

"Did you miss me?" Bailey asked, cuddling the little dog, reveling in the unconditional love.

"You didn't miss her, did you, Samantha?" Jodi scratched the animal behind one pointy, tufted ear. "She's only pretending to be ecstatic. A good job of it, too, Samantha."

"Want to go for a *walk*?" Bailey asked, stressing the last word. Samantha wriggled out of her arms, jumped to the floor, and began running in circles, yipping and waving her plumed tail.

"I'd say that's a definite yes," Jodi interpreted, tossing her handbag onto the glass-topped coffee table. "Poor thing's probably been standing around for hours with her legs crossed."

Bailey withdrew a lavender halter and leash from the coat closet and held it close to the floor. Samantha lowered her head and charged directly into the opening, dancing up and down impatiently while Bailey fastened the buckle and laughed at Samantha's enthusiasm.

"Come on," she called to Jodi. "This is a great way to meet your new neighbors. Samantha knows everybody."

As the trio proceeded across the grounds, the little

dog pranced along, sniffed shrubs, trees, and flowers, and stopped to say hello to everyone. After Jodi had inquired as to the identity of the third man they met, Bailey finally asked her, "Do you want me to have a party and invite all the males I know, however remotely, so you can meet them?"

"That's a good idea," Jodi agreed. "You're just wasting them."

A high-pitched voice interrupted. "Look, Pumpkin. There's that cute little dog again." A white toy poodle and matching owner bounced up to greet Samantha. "What kind of dog did you say she is?" Pumpkin's leash holder asked.

"A Chorkie," Bailey replied, ignoring Jodi's coughing spasm.

The woman nodded sagely. "They're such a cute breed. I almost got one before I found Pumpkin."

The dogs sniffed each other briefly, then led their owners on to seek more interesting smells.

"Chorkie?" Jodi questioned when the pair had moved a few bushes away.

"Yorkie/Chihuahua. What do you want me to say she is, a Yihuahua? That lady'll tell all her friends about seeing a Chorkie, and they'll all pretend to know what she's talking about. They'll probably go to the pet store and ask for one. But there's only one Samantha, isn't there, sweetheart?" She reached down to scratch the little head as Samantha bent over a tuft of grass, sniffing in absorption.

"Hey, Ms. Attorney-at-Law, what would your new friend, Austin Travers, think if he saw you goo-gooing over a dog?"

"*Your* new friend would be jealous because I have a Chorkie, and he doesn't."

"Jealous? No, I can't see that. Though if there were only one Chorkie in the world and he wanted it, I can see him moving heaven and hell to get it."

Bailey scowled at her friend, but didn't deny the

accuracy of her assessment. Austin's competitive nature—Austin's ability to win—both excited and frightened her. A tingle raced along her spine as she recalled the fierce competition of the race.

Mostly, she had to admit, it excited her.

TWO

"Good morning, Joan." Bailey greeted the receptionist, picked up her messages, and thumbed through them as she strode down the hall. Dressed in a tailored black suit with a white silk blouse, still exhilarated by the race on Saturday, she felt ready to take on the world, even Stafford Morris.

As she passed the large conference room, the door opened and Lisa Palmer, one of the secretaries, came out. Bailey had only a quick glimpse of the interior of the room before the door closed, but it was enough to pull her up short, suddenly alert.

"Lisa, who's in there?" she asked.

In that brief instant, she'd seen a familiar head bent over the polished wood of the conference table, a head with black, razor-cut hair. Unlikely as the possibility seemed, it was even more unlikely she'd hallucinate Austin Travers.

"We're deposing Candy Miller," Lisa answered. "You know, that personal injury suit Margaret got stuck with."

Bailey vaguely remembered that Margaret Hodges had asked her a couple of questions concerning the legalities, but details of the case escaped her. "Who's counsel for the insurance company?"

"Mark Powell at Kearns, Worley, Lewis, Hooper and Day."

Austin's firm. "Is Mark Powell the man with dark hair sitting at this end of the table?" she asked, though she already knew what the answer would be.

"Oh, no. Mr. Powell's at the far end. He's short and blond. That other guy's some big gun from the Kearns branch in St. Louis. I don't know who he is, but Margaret had me serve coffee in our real cups. Mark Powell only rates paper cups."

"Thanks, Lisa." Bailey turned back to her message slips and continued down the hall, but she wasn't reading the names and phone numbers in front of her. It *was* him—in her office, her territory. A brief, titillating fantasy flashed unbidden through her mind—of the two of them going head to head in the courtroom.

She entered her office and slid into her soft gray chair behind the desk she'd chosen for its smooth walnut top, a top she hadn't seen since the day the desk arrived. Someday she'd have to peek under the mounds of paper just to be sure it was still there.

Sorting the new message slips in order of how soon, if ever, the call should be returned, she added them to an existing pile on her desk, then scowled at the one on top. Larry Haynes would expect to hear from her ten minutes ago. She had nothing new to tell him on the lease she was negotiating for him, but the man wanted his attorneys to jump on command. He was rich, rude, and obnoxious. She moved his message to the middle of the pile.

Her mind jumped back to the unresolved question of Austin's presence. Why would a "big gun" get involved in a simple personal injury lawsuit, one her firm had assigned to a second-year associate? Could the insurance company Kearns, Worley was representing possibly be that important? If so, why was Mark Powell, a fairly new associate, the official attorney of record? Was that only a smoke screen so they could slip something past her firm?

As she recalled, her firm's client, the woman being deposed, had the infamous, unprovable "back injury." Therefore, it was simply a matter of negotiating a settlement with the insurance company that would be less than the woman deserved if she was really injured and more than she deserved if she was faking.

"Where's that damned Gordon?" The voice charged into her office along with its owner.

"Good morning, Stafford. How are you?" Bailey replied.

"I'd be a hell of a lot better if people could get to work on time," he grumbled.

Bailey rose from her chair, aware that her two-inch heels put her at eye level with Stafford Morris and cut down on his intimidation factor, his strong point. A very bald head accentuated his large nose and stubborn chin, and he walked with his head thrust forward, as though daring anyone to get in his way. They rarely did.

"The next time it's my week to watch Gordon, I'll see to it he gets here early every morning," she assured him sarcastically.

"I want him in my office as soon as he gets in." Morris stalked to her door, then turned back. "I hear you did all right at the race Saturday."

"Nothing spectacular." But she smiled in spite of herself, not only about the race but also because Morris didn't add the phrase "for a woman" to the end of his sentence. It had taken her a long time to achieve that omission.

Morris nodded, and Bailey thought his mouth curved upward fractionally just before he turned to leave her office.

"I saw an acquaintance of yours at the race," she

called after him. "Austin Travers with Kearns, Worley."

Morris looked back at her, his face unreadable. "Is that right?"

"Good runner."

"Hmmph."

"Why's he involved in that personal injury case Margaret Hodges got stuck with?"

"What makes you think he is?"

"He's in the conference room, taking Candy Miller's deposition."

Morris' eyes narrowed speculatively. He reached into his jacket pocket for a cigar. "Interesting."

Bailey watched as he charged off down the hall. Gordon was right. The man deserved to have Jodi as his secretary. But did Jodi deserve Stafford Morris?

That afternoon Bailey made it a point to visit Margaret's office. "How'd your deposition go this morning?" she asked, peering around the doorway into the small space. As a second-year associate, Margaret didn't get a window.

"Okay, I guess." Margaret shrugged. Her round face projected youth and insecurity in spite of large, black-framed glasses and pale hair pulled back into a tight bun.

"Heard the opposition brought in reinforcements," Bailey said, sliding into one of the client chairs in front of Margaret's desk.

"Yeah, that was kinda strange. Some heavy hitter from the branch office in St. Louis."

"I thought this case was pretty routine. Why did they have a 'heavy hitter' here? What did he do in there?"

Margaret shuffled the papers on her desk. "Mostly he just watched everybody, like he could see right through us. But then sometimes he'd come up with a question we'd never thought of. He got Candy really flustered a couple of times."

Bailey leaned forward. "Do you think he's planning

to take this thing to trial? Is the insurance company a major client for them? Is our client's credibility bad?''

"I don't know. Candy's okay. She's not real smart, but that doesn't have anything to do with her legal rights.''

But in the hands of a slick lawyer, it might have a lot to do with the way she came across to a jury, Bailey reflected. And if Austin was as good in the courtroom as he was on the track—

"What's next on the agenda?'' Bailey asked.

Margaret checked her desk calendar. "Depositions for the insurance company and their investigator next Monday morning, nine o'clock.''

"If you'd like me to go along for a little backup, I'd be happy to,'' Bailey offered, trying to sound nonchalant, as though she could care less what Margaret's answer was. Leaving Margaret to go up against Austin alone was like throwing a Christian to the lions. Bailey owed it to her firm to see that they were adequately represented, she assured herself virtuously.

Tiny tension lines on Margaret's face suddenly relaxed. "If you have time, that would be great.''

Bailey stood to leave. "Fine. Get me the file as soon as you can, and the deposition the minute we receive it.''

A heavy hitter, Bailey mused as she strode down the carpeted hallway. *A big gun.* A big egomaniac. That's what he was. Come to town and get involved in an insignificant case. Try to intimidate her firm's client, not to mention the attorney from her firm. Well, if he wanted intimidation, she'd teach him the meaning of the word.

"Bailey!'' Gordon greeted, appearing beside her and breaking into her thoughts. "I think there's a law against looking that happy while you're still at work.''

"Happy?'' She tried to scowl away the smile, though she couldn't deny to herself that she was looking forward to another encounter with Austin.

She turned into the kitchen, followed by Gordon, and selected a soda from the vending machine. "Why is Austin Travers involved in the *Miller v. National Service Insurance* case?" she asked.

"I didn't know he was." Gordon poured himself a cup of black, dense coffee and added several packets of sugar.

"I can't believe you're going to drink that."

"I'm not," Gordon assured her. "I'm going to eat it. Speaking of which, what are you doing for dinner tonight?" He stirred his nauseating concoction and actually took a sip.

"Nothing. Want to grab a bite?" Bailey tilted her head back for a long drink of her cool, effervescent liquid.

"Sure. Austin's meeting me over at Reilly's at seven-thirty. Even you should be finished working by then, and you can ask Austin whatever it is you want to know about him."

Bailey almost choked on her drink. "Oh, no. I wouldn't intrude on your evening with your friend." Racing with him, meeting him in the courtroom—that was one thing, but no way did she want to be in a social setting with Austin Travers.

"You're my friend, too," Gordon assured her, "so you'll be Austin's friend."

"Maybe another time."

"You're not feeling awkward about going out with two men, are you, Bailey? Hey, I always think of you as just one of the boys, you know." He winked and punched her shoulder in mock camaraderie. "See you tonight, buddy." He strolled out.

"Don't wait dinner on me," Bailey called after him.

Still, as the day wore on, she found herself questioning her decision. She'd gone out with Gordon and his friends before. She was never uncomfortable dealing with men on a friendship basis. Why was Austin different?

Irritably she thumped the eraser end of a pencil on her desktop. Why *was* Austin different?

She didn't still resent him for using her to get next to Jodi since he didn't seem to be making any real efforts in that direction. And the days were long past when she'd been prone to losing the power of speech if a good-looking male smiled at her.

For that matter, Austin wasn't any better-looking than Gordon. He did have a nicer body, more muscular. And his dark hair and burning eyes made a striking contrast. His features were more irregular than Gordon's, too, more interesting.

None of which explained why she was so reluctant to meet him and Gordon for dinner. She realized the tempo of her pencil tapping had increased measurably, and forced herself to stop.

Very well, she decided, since there was no logical reason not to go to dinner with Gordon and Austin, she'd be there.

Austin leaned back in the dim, cool booth at Reilly's and smiled politely when Gordon told him Bailey would be joining them for dinner. But his feelings were ambivalent. True, the idea of seeing her again brought every nerve ending in his body to attention, but he'd wanted to relax for the evening. Bailey was definitely not a soothing influence.

As he went into his second week at the Kansas City office, the problems and stress had mounted in direct proportion to his discovery of the situation. Everyone, even the lawyers, were perfectly happy with the status quo. Growth, expansion, updating, only meant change and uncertainty to them. In particular, the partners who were senior to him were making it difficult. Though he was attempting to carry out the majority decision, they acted as if he had no authority.

Spending time alone with Gordon would be restorative. Having Bailey around would be almost as stress-

ful as trying to iron out the problems at work. Still, the
idea also held a certain amount of pleasurable excita-
tion, a large amount, in fact. He adapted to the confusing situation by ordering a second Scotch on the rocks.

"I just hope she gets here soon," he told Gordon.
"I'm starving. Didn't have time for lunch."

Gordon shook his head. "You seem to have a problem keeping your priorities straight," he drawled, sipping lazily on his beer. "I always have time for lunch.
It's the work I sometimes have to put aside."

"You haven't changed a bit in twenty years." Austin
grinned in spite of himself.

"Haven't seen any reason to change. I like me this
way. Maybe I don't have any ambition, but hey, that's
okay. I have lots of money in my trust fund. It seems
a shame to let it all go to waste."

"But you're wasting yourself. You're a talented attorney. Hell, just the fact that you manage to keep your
job with that old Scrooge shows you must be doing
something right. If you put forth even a little effort,
you'd make partner." He accepted his drink from the
waitress, took a quick sip, and set it on the table, wrapping both hands around the cool glass.

Propping one elbow on the back of the booth, Gordon smiled lazily. "Let's say I work harder and make
partner; then I'd have to work even harder, and for
what? I don't need the money. So I'd work more, play
less, put more money in the bank for my heirs at law
to fight over when I'm dead, which would be a lot
sooner under those circumstances—nah, I don't think I
want to be partner this week."

"Gordon, you're hopeless."

Gordon shrugged unrepentantly and had another
drink of beer.

Austin wrapped his fingers around his glass, but
stopped before raising it to his lips as the atmosphere
in the room seemed to change, to become charged with
energy. *Ridiculous*. But he wasn't surprised to see Bai-

ley approaching. For an instant their gazes met, but before he could read her expression, she lowered her eyes and slid into the booth next to Gordon.

"Just get off work?" Gordon asked.

"No, I went home to feed Samantha—my dog," she explained with a quick, neutral glance in Austin's direction. "Then Jodi called while I was there."

"Hasn't changed her mind, has she?" Gordon inquired, a trace of concern in his voice.

"Oh, no," Bailey replied, and Austin was sure she'd missed the nuance. "In one more week she'll be an employee of Hoskins, Grier and Morris, God rest her soul."

"And a roommate of Bailey Russell, ditto," Gordon added.

"Hold your tongue or I'll tell Stafford where you go to nap."

After they placed their orders, Austin cast about for something to say to Bailey. Everything that came to mind, he discarded. The standard small talk wouldn't do. She'd just look at him with that clear green gaze and make some satirical comment that cut right through the nonsense.

"I did stay a little late at the office," she said abruptly, fixing him with that gaze he'd been thinking about. "An important case like *Miller v. National Service Insurance* justifies some overtime. Wouldn't you agree, Austin?"

He stared at her uncomprehendingly for a moment. Why did she have an interest in that case? She wasn't the assigned attorney. And why had she said it was important? It appeared to be relatively insignificant. He'd decided, after going through the deposition with Mark Powell today, that Mark was competent enough to handle it. The boy could use a few lessons on power techniques, but power hadn't seemed necessary in that instance. After Bailey's remark, though, he'd have to keep an eye on that deal.

"Makes sense to me," he finally said, deliberately being as evasive as possible. Not the answer she'd wanted, he could tell. Her eyes narrowed, and her lips compressed slightly.

"Of course, one never knows the full magnitude of any situation until all the facts are out in the open."

What on earth was she talking about? "Volcanoes frequently erupt with very little warning." There. That should give her something to think about.

"And how was your day, Gordon?" Gordon interrupted. "Oh, the usual. I won a case in Supreme Court, wrote a lease that Larry Haynes liked on the first draft, and Stafford Morris told me I'm a great lawyer. Just your average Monday."

"Aren't you getting enough attention?" Bailey asked, wrapping a long, slim arm around his neck.

With a shock, the idea hit Austin that Bailey and Gordon might be lovers. Impossible! Gordon had never mentioned it, and besides, how could anyone so easy-going be attracted to someone so pushy? Though she actually looked soft as she kissed Gordon's cheek, those enormous eyes half-closed, her full lips pursed.

Gordon smiled smugly. "Are you taking notes?" he asked. "How to get a beautiful woman's attention."

"Gordon," Bailey said, laughing and pushing him away, "if you weren't my friend, I wouldn't even like you."

They weren't lovers, Austin decided with an inexplicable rush of relief.

Friday afternoon Bailey was working frantically on a project that had to go out with the Federal Express pickup at six when Gordon strolled into her office and flopped into a chair.

"What's up?" she asked, never lifting her eyes from the papers strewn across her desk, tactfully letting him know she didn't have time to talk.

"TGIF, Bailey, my friend. What's on your agenda for the weekend?"

"Not much. Jodi's moving in tomorrow."

"Don't tell me you're taking Saturday off."

Bailey looked up briefly to smile. "What an imagination you have."

"So your friend's going to be stuck by herself in a strange city, unloading furniture and heavy boxes."

Bailey looked up again. Gordon had swung one leg over the arm of his chair and was helping himself to a mint from the jar on her desk.

"What is this, Gordon?" she asked. "Are you strapped for entertainment? Are all your girlfriends out of town for the weekend? Are you hinting for an invitation? Okay. Jodi's storing her furniture, but why don't you go over and help her unload boxes, and when I get there, we'll all have pizza and beer and watch video-taped segments of *L.A. Law*. Now go away and let me work."

Gordon rose with a sigh, returning the candy jar to her desk. "I'm a busy man, but no one could resist such a gracious invitation. I'll baby-sit Jodi and Samantha until you make it home, then keep you girls company for the rest of the evening."

Bailey smiled to herself as Gordon strolled away. His friendship meant a lot to her, and she was glad he and Jodi seemed to get along so well. She'd try a little harder to get along with his friend Austin. The guy wasn't all bad. He was, after all, a good runner with great legs.

And wouldn't he be surprised when she showed up at that deposition on Monday. That whole situation was still a mystery to her. After going over the entire file and Candy Miller's deposition, she could see no reason for Austin's intrusion into the case, or for that matter, her own. Except something was going on, and she owed it to her firm to find out what.

But that was Monday. She pushed aside the pleasurable anticipation. Right now she had to finish the blasted contract.

When Bailey arrived home early Saturday afternoon, she noticed several cardboard boxes in the spare room, but no bodies. Even Samantha was gone. However, stuck to the refrigerator door she found a small, yellow note with the single word "Pool" scrawled in Gordon's inimitable handwriting.

As she started to leave the room, she spotted a newspaper lying on the kitchen counter, folded over to the classifieds, with one ad circled in red.

"I've kissed the requisite number of frogs," she read, "so where is Prince Charming? PC is tall (even without the crown), intelligent, and easy on the eyes. His Cinderella is slim, five feet four when not wearing her glass slippers, dark hair and eyes. She'd love to go to the ball or even the local Burger King with the real PC or a reasonable facsimile thereof. No lawyers need apply."

Bailey wondered briefly what her chances were of finding and burning every copy of the paper before Jodi got herself in trouble.

Slipping on an old swimsuit and half a bottle of sunscreen to avoid the freckles that had been the bane of her younger years, she headed for the pool to find the three of them and see how much trouble they were in already.

As she rounded the building and approached the pool, she saw Gordon and Jodi lying stretched out full length, almost visibly turning brown in the warm sun. Beside them, Samantha lay on her back in Austin Travers' lap, looking up at him with adoring brown eyes while he scratched her stomach.

For an instant she panicked. What was he doing here? Gordon could at least have given her a little warning, a chance to get prepared. Squaring her shoulders and wishing she had on a business suit rather than a swimsuit, she opened the gate and strode determinedly toward them.

Austin could feel himself unwinding as he soaked up the warm sun, enjoyed the nondemanding companionship of Jodi and Gordon, and stroked Samantha's soft, fuzzy stomach. Anxious to get out of the tiny apartment where he'd been staying, he'd agreed to come along with Gordon and help Jodi move some boxes upstairs to Bailey's condo.

He stopped scratching Samantha's stomach just to make her raise one little paw toward his hand, silently urging him to keep moving. But this time she stopped, paw half-raised, rolled to her feet, and dashed out of his lap.

He made a futile grab for her leash, then looked up to see Bailey gliding toward him. The faded black swimsuit she wore emphasized her translucent skin and hugged her streamlined curves. Smiling broadly, she stooped to catch the little dog in midjump.

The sight brought out the usual mixed feelings he'd come to associate with Bailey. On the one hand, he wanted to touch her porcelain skin, see if it really was as smooth as it looked. On the other hand, he felt the need to stand up before her and prepare for battle.

Choosing a third option, he employed the smile that showed his molars. "Bailey! How nice you look."

Gordon and Jodi opened their eyes and sat up.

Bailey looked at everyone, then turned her gaze back to him. "Why, thank you, Austin. How kind of you to say so."

"Bailey, have a beer," Gordon offered, opening an ice chest. "Anybody else ready for another?"

"I saw your ad," Bailey said to Jodi, accepting the can and settling herself into their midst, folding her long legs under her sleek body.

"What do you think?" Jodi asked. "I wrote it kind of fast so I could get it in this edition."

"Oh, it was well written. You always were very articulate."

"Quite creative, I thought," Gordon added. "I told her she ought to try for a career as a writer, but—" he shrugged and rolled his eyes "—you know how dedicated she is to being a legal secretary."

Jodi pressed her cold beer against Gordon's back, eliciting a brief shriek. Everyone laughed, but a loud silence followed. Soft laps of water against the side of the pool and muted music from someone's radio sounded clearly.

Austin was trying to decide if perhaps he ought to leave since Bailey hadn't invited him, and it was, after all, her place, when she turned to him. Her hundred-watt smile set every nerve in his body to jangling in excitement and apprehension.

"You will stay for pizza this evening, won't you? Or do you have plans?"

How tactful. Straight out of a textbook on manners. He could match that. "Thank you," he said. "I'd love to stay."

"Good deal," Gordon approved. "You can carry the pizza, and Samantha'll probably let you rub her tummy some more."

Jodi reached over to stroke the fuzzy head as Samantha looked up at the mention of her name. "She took an immediate liking to him," she informed Bailey. "Jumped into his arms the minute he walked through the gate."

Everyone smiled. Gordon and Jodi smeared on more suntan oil and stretched out.

Austin reached over and scratched behind Samantha's ears, accidentally brushing Bailey's hand in the process. Her skin was smooth and firm and warm.

"We always had big dogs," he said, jerking back, pretending he hadn't noticed the contact.

"We?" she asked. If it had been any other woman, he'd have thought she was trying to find out if he was married. However, he felt sure Bailey was simply requesting information.

"My family," he told her. "Not me. I don't have time to care for an animal. Besides, my town house in St. Louis is no place for a Doberman."

Bailey nodded. "I feel guilty about leaving Samantha alone all day. Sometimes I take her to the office with me on Saturdays."

"You're kidding! What does Stafford Morris say about that?"

"He doesn't. The view of the office is a little obscured from his golf course at the country club."

Austin laughed delightedly at Bailey's sardonic humor. Her mouth quirked upward, and those incredible sea green eyes danced.

"How about a swim?" he asked, suddenly unable to sit still. "The sun's getting pretty hot."

"Jodi, can you hold Samantha?" She turned the leash over to her friend, who accepted it without opening her eyes.

The pool was a decent size, as condo pools went. The space appeared more than adequate for its purpose since most of the residents were lying beside it. Only four other people were actually in the pool, including one tan lady floating lazily on a raft. Austin almost sighed as the cool water enveloped his overheated body. The day had turned into a scorcher.

Beside him Bailey slid completely under the water and came up, shaking her short hair. Not many women could still look good with no makeup and wet hair, Austin thought, falling into a leisurely backstroke, watching Bailey as she joined him.

At the end of the pool, they turned and launched into a crawl simultaneously, laughing at the coincidence. Bailey was a relatively strong swimmer, Austin thought. She didn't seem to have any problem keeping up with him. They hit the other end and flipped over.

Austin stretched out, reaching, feeling the rush of

adrenaline from exercise. Through the churning water, he could see Bailey beside him, and they shared a smile. Austin increased his stroke. They hit the opposite end at the same time.

Of course, Bailey would be faster than most women. She had nothing on that sleek body to slow her down. Even her small, high breasts appeared aerodynamically designed.

Damn her, he thought, stroking as hard as he could, hitting the end of the pool and flipping back the other way, didn't she know he was physically stronger than she was? Hadn't he proven that at the run?

"Get out of the pool," he heard someone shout, and looked up to see Gordon and Jodi on the edge, glaring down.

Were they crazy? He was pulling ahead of Bailey. He wasn't about to get out now.

They bounced off the edge and started another lap. He'd pass her for sure this time. Again and again his arm raised out of the cool water into the warm sun, back into the cool. His muscles stretched, lengthened, contracted. He couldn't see Bailey from the corner of his eye anymore. He'd passed her! He was winning!

A hand grabbed his as he neared the end of the pool again. "If you don't get out of the pool, I'll throw in your Cartier," Gordon promised, dangling the watch over the water with his other hand.

Austin stared uncomprehendingly at his friend's face, at Bailey pulling up beside him. Damn! She hadn't been very far behind, but with a few more laps . . . . Were Gordon and Jodi conspiring to keep him from winning?

"Why?" he demanded angrily.

"Look around you," Jodi invited. "You've succeeded in clearing the pool. You've embarrassed even Gordon and me, and that isn't easy to do."

Austin looked. The bronzed lady clutched her raft and glared. He and Bailey were the only ones in the water. Reluctantly he pulled himself up. Bailey followed suit, and they sat on the concrete rim, breathing hard, staring across the water. Jodi and Gordon moved back to the ice chest, and he heard a beer can pop.

"Pretend you don't know them," Jodi advised from the background.

I won, Austin wanted to shout. *I was ahead when they stopped us.* He couldn't say that. They hadn't been racing. "You're a good swimmer," he said, grudgingly.

"Thanks. So are you," she replied. Her response wasn't very hearty either.

"Don't feel badly because I was ahead of you. Men are inherently physically stronger than women." There! He'd managed to remind her of his victory by putting it on an impersonal basis. Just a simple statement of biological fact.

"That's true," she agreed sweetly, green eyes dancing. "It's Mother Nature's vain attempt at compensation for shorting men in the brains department."

THREE.

Bailey opened her briefcase and laid a couple of file folders along with a yellow legal pad on the conference room table at Kearns, Worley's law offices.

"Nothing for me," she told the secretary taking coffee orders. She didn't need any caffeine. She was wide-awake.

In fact, she was experiencing some distinctly odd sensations not usually associated with taking a deposition, including an impulse to bolt out of her chair and do some stretching exercises, take a few deep breaths, gear up for a race.

Of course, this was business, not a race. She knew that.

The door whispered open, the faint sound demanding Bailey's attention. Her heartbeat accelerated perceptibly as she looked up, then returned to normal when the secretary came into the room bearing a tray of steaming cups.

Sitting next to her, Margaret accepted coffee. "Thank you," she mumbled, then gave one final blot with a crumpled tissue to her pale, damp forehead.

Not all the perspiration came from anxiety, Bailey reflected. Margaret and Candy Miller, the client, had puffed their way to the office building, though it was only two blocks from their own. Bailey had had to stop every few steps and wait for them to catch up.

No wonder Candy's back hurt. Bailey watched the woman accept a cup of coffee with cream and sugar. She was in lousy physical condition. Cellulitic breasts protruding above the open buttons of her purple blouse bounced on her stomach. A good bra and a healthy diet would probably solve most of her back problem.

She pulled her attention away from the woman, mentally rebuking herself for her unkind thoughts. Just because she herself was obsessed with physical fitness didn't mean everyone else should be.

Thoughts of physical fitness returned her focus to Austin. The door opened again, but it was only the secretary leaving.

Bailey drummed her fingers impatiently. The court reporter was there, Mark Powell was there, the insured, Alvin Wilson, was there, the men from the insurance company were there—but Austin Travers was noticeably absent. They began the deposition.

The testimonies of Alvin Wilson and the insurance company representative were brief and unremarkable. Alvin had rear-ended Candy at a red light. Responsibility clearly lay with the defendant. The extent of Candy's injury was the sole issue in dispute. Able to contribute only a few pertinent questions, Bailey had begun to doubt the necessity of her presence when Mark excused himself and left the room. Bailey waited impatiently for his return, bored and anxious to get the proceeding over with.

Then the door swung open and Austin Travers surged in, impressive in a gray pinstripe suit only a few shades darker than her own. As he entered, the air in the room seemed suddenly charged, alive.

His electric blue gaze swept the room, zoomed in on Bailey. She'd heard of auras surrounding people, but had never given the idea any credence. Nevertheless, she could have sworn an aura crackled around Austin's head. The hair on her arms stood up inside her white blouse. She felt alive and vibrant, eager to get on with things, to engage in battle.

Austin sensed a rush of unleashed energy as he stepped into the conference room where Bailey Russell waited, her svelte body hidden by a tailored gray suit. She looked up at him, her eyes wide pools of innocence, as though her mere presence weren't an alert that something was going on. Deliberately he looked away from her, reached for the knob to close the door behind Mark, jumped as static electricity sparked to his hand. For a brief, illogical moment, he blamed—or credited—Bailey.

"How nice to see you, Mr. Travers." Her voice was deceptive, a soothing cello in the supercharged atmosphere.

"Ms. Russell. I didn't expect to see you here."

She smiled sweetly, savagely. What on earth was she up to? From what he had observed and Mark had told him, the case involved no special circumstances. Yet Bailey had brought it up when she'd met Gordon and him at Reilly's, had called it "important," and now she'd come to the deposition and so intimidated Mark that he'd felt it necessary to seek Austin's advice.

Austin took over. Mark had briefed him on the situation prior to Candy Miller's deposition, and he knew that the testimony of Harold Graham, the investigator, should put an end to her claims. He put the witness through his paces, established the fact that Graham had been observing her periodically for several weeks, cited inconsequential activities such as working in her yard or taking out the trash. Then he moved in for the kill.

"You are aware that the plaintiff is claiming loss of income in her profession of cocktail waitress due to this injury."

"Yes."

"Please tell us what happened on the evening of June twelfth."

"That'd be Friday week ago?"

"Right."

"Well, she gets all dolled up and goes down to this bar where she used to work. She's been there several times already, so I follow her, like I've done before. Friday nights are real crowded, and next thing I know, she's up hustling drinks."

"You actually saw her serve drinks to customers?"

"Hell, she served me."

"What kind of shoes was she wearing?"

"Red sandals with real high heels."

"Did she exhibit any signs of difficulty in walking, such as limping, clutching her back, moving slowly?"

"Nope. She was whipping around pretty good."

"Did she grimace, groan, give any evidence of being in pain?"

"Nope. In fact, she was laughing and having a big time."

Austin stole a look in Bailey's direction and made a mental note never to play poker with her. She was observing dispassionately, not even bothering to take written notes.

"May we have a couple of minutes to confer with our client before cross-examination?" she asked smoothly when Austin passed the witness.

The three of them were out of the room less than five minutes, during which time Candy, wearing thick glasses, stuck her head back in the door once, peered at Harold, then retreated. When they returned, Bailey, rather than Margaret, took charge, as he'd suspected she would. Standing directly across the table from the witness, she began to question him in a quiet voice.

"Did you actually see Candy Miller accept drinks from the bartender and serve them to customers?" she asked after a few preliminary innocuous questions.

Austin watched Harold's complacent expression. The

man was too macho to be frightened of a woman. Austin tried to catch his eye, to warn him to be on his guard, but Harold was smiling stupidly at Bailey.

"She served me," he drawled.

"What kind of a drink? Big? Little?" The volume and speed of her words increased, and she somehow gave the impression of becoming taller.

"Seven and Seven. Big glass." He seemed hypnotized by her steady gaze, unable to look away from her.

"How many other tables did she serve?"

"A couple."

"You saw no visible signs of any ill effects from this stint of working?" Her voice was rising and speeding up again.

"Nope."

"Not at any time during the evening?"

"Nope."

"How many times did you follow Candy to this club?"

"A couple."

"More than one."

"Sure."

"More than two."

"Yeah, probably."

"Three? Four?"

"I guess."

"How long did she usually stay?"

"Until midnight, two o'clock."

"And you only saw her wait tables the one time?"

"Isn't that enough?"

"Of course," Bailey agreed, her voice suddenly soothing again. Harold grinned proudly. Austin groaned silently.

The air in the room seemed so charged with trapped electricity, Austin half expected to see lightning flash over the table. *Watch out*, he wanted to warn Graham.

"So you went to the same bar as the plaintiff on three or four occasions, stayed until she left, and watched her carefully the entire time." She looked down at the table, shuffled through some papers, released Harold from her gaze.

"Sure did."

Austin watched in fascination. She was moving in for the kill.

She abandoned the papers and fixed her attention on Graham again. "What time did she arrive at the club on the night in question?"

"Four minutes till nine."

"You're a very precise man, Mr. Graham."

Harold shrugged happily at the compliment. "Just part of the job."

"And what time did the alleged incident occur?"

"Around midnight."

"Can you be more precise?"

"Midnight, give or take a few minutes."

"How many drinks did the plaintiff have before this time?"

"Several."

"More than a couple?"

"Six, seven."

"You've testified that she had no difficulty walking. Did she not show any signs of intoxication after all that alcohol?"

"Well, she may have swayed a little, and she talked kinda slurred and laughed awful loud."

"So when you testified before that she was 'whipping around pretty good,' that wasn't completely accurate."

"Well, you know, not limping or anything. Maybe swaying a little."

"I see. What, exactly, did she say when she volunteered to help out at the bar?"

"I didn't exactly hear her say anything. I just saw her go up to the bar, pick up a tray, and start serving."

"How many drinks were on her tray when she left the bar?"

"I couldn't see for sure. The place was crowded. A

lot, probably. She stopped at a couple of tables before she got to me.'' Harold was starting to squirm.

The air conditioning kicked on, and Austin jumped, the sound seeming as loud as thunder. He leaned back, hungry for the cool.

"How many Seven and Sevens had you had by this time?''

"A couple.''

"Mr. Graham, could you be more precise in your definition of the phrase 'a couple'? You seem to use this term rather vaguely.''

"Two or three, maybe.''

"Four or five?''

"Maybe four. I couldn't sit there all night and not order. They'd've run me out.''

"I understand. But can we assume that between the dim light, the crowd, and 'a couple' of drinks, you have no idea how many drinks were on the plaintiff's tray when she left the bar?''

"Yeah, I guess so.''

"Then you can only say for certain that she had one drink on her tray, namely, your Seven and Seven?''

"Why would she stop at those other tables if she wasn't giving them drinks?''

"Since you testified she's a regular, perhaps she was chatting with friends. Did she talk to the people at the tables?''

Harold ducked his head and mumbled something.

"I missed that, Mr. Graham.''

"I dunno. Maybe.'' He straightened. "But she musta been serving drinks, too.''

"How much did she charge you for your drink?''

Harold mumbled again.

"Please speak up, Mr. Graham. These proceedings are being recorded.''

"I said, nothing.''

"Nothing. Had you been receiving free drinks all evening?''

"No."

"Yet the house bought that particular drink for you?"

"No. Not the house. She did."

"Did she give you a reason for that unusual act?"

Harold looked at the ceiling and sighed, an act of resignation.

Austin could have sworn he saw tiny sparks jumping from Bailey's fiery hair.

"She said it was to cure my shyness, that she'd seen me watching her before and knew I wanted to meet her."

"Thank you, Mr. Graham. That'll be all. I'm sure we can dispense with any further details."

"There aren't any more details!"

"Thank you. That'll be all."

And that, Austin mused, was definitely all. So much for Harold Graham's testimony. Austin was furious. He wanted to swear. Conversely, he had to duck his head to hide a smile. That was crazy. How could he smile when Bailey had just blown away their witness? Was it possible to admire someone's expertise with a knife when your own throat was being slit?

"What do we do now?" Mark asked him as everyone shoved back their chairs and prepared to depart.

"We congratulate the opposition," Austin replied, and moved around to catch Bailey before she could get out the door.

"Well done," he murmured, extending his hand.

She raised an eyebrow, shifted her briefcase, and slid her long, slim fingers into his. Static electricity jumped between them, and they gasped, then laughed nervously. Austin shook her hand, then held it, surprised at the fragile feel of fingers that could probably crush an anvil.

With a shock, Austin recognized a stirring in his groin that couldn't possibly be happening under such circumstances.

"Good job," he said, releasing her hand and backing away, stuffing his own hands in his pockets to obscure the evidence.

"Good-bye," he said, and bolted from the room.

"You were fantastic!" Margaret praised as they walked back to the office. "You made a fool out of that man."

Bailey stepped off the curb and frowned into the sun. "He seemed a little upset, but I certainly wouldn't describe him as a fool."

"No, Margaret's right, he looked really dumb," Candy contributed, puffing a little. "When you made him admit the only drink I carried was to him, his face got all red."

"Oh. Yes, well, I guess that's true." Bailey had assumed they were talking about Austin. She had momentarily forgotten that anyone else had been there.

"They'll be calling us before the day's over to offer a settlement," Margaret declared, almost bouncing down the sidewalk.

"And this'll be all over?" Candy questioned.

"No way," Bailey said, pushing through the revolving door into the office building.

"Why?" Candy asked, following her.

"The first offer is only an opening gambit. Don't worry. We'll go to court if they don't offer enough."

"But what if they offer enough?" Candy tripped along on her stiletto heels, trying to keep up.

"If they offer enough, we'll take it," Bailey reassured her. "But they won't."

"Let's go to lunch and celebrate," Margaret proposed.

"You two go ahead," Bailey declined. "I have plans."

She watched the pair totter away, then went upstairs to find Jodi and see how she was surviving her first day.

At the end of the office hallway, outside Stafford Morris' corner office, Bailey leaned over the side of the modular cubicle. Jodi sat facing a word processor, dictation earphones disappearing under her curls, fingers flying over the keyboard.

"You're still here," Bailey said.

Peeling off the phones, Jodi turned to face her. "Back already? How'd the big deposition go? Was Austin impressive?"

Impressive? Yes, she thought. Austin was, to say the least, impressive. "I won," she said, ignoring Jodi's last question.

Jodi grinned. "You won? I didn't know this was a contest."

"I didn't say it was a contest, but certainly there are winners and losers in every legal battle. And I won this round."

"You mean your client won."

Bailey straightened up and folded her arms. "I won for our client. Look, I came back here to ask you if you wanted to go to lunch, but I'm about to change my mind. I was even going to offer to pay, and we could go somewhere with a menu on the table instead of the wall."

Jodi crinkled her nose. "Thanks, but Mr. Morris has some clients in his office, and he wants me to go get sandwiches for everybody, then kind of hang around while I eat mine in case he needs me."

"Good grief." Bailey cast a malevolent glance at Stafford Morris' closed door. "I'd think the old goat would cut you a little slack on your first day."

"Quite the opposite, actually. There's a backlog of things his temp didn't do that he wants me to catch up on."

"Oh, well. I guess I'll just go downstairs and get ptomaine poisoning. How's it going otherwise? Has he blown cigar smoke in your face yet?"

Jodi laughed. "Once, but I blew it back at him."

Bailey looked heavenward. "Why doesn't that surprise me?"

Jodi held her earphones out, ready to pop them into her ears. "Get out of here or I'll take your name off the list for the fiscal-year-end party next month."

Bailey grimaced. "Oh, yes, you do have the honor of planning that mess, don't you?"

"Mess? You're spoiled. A Las Vegas party on a riverboat cruising down the Missouri River sounds like a blast to me."

Stafford Morris' door suddenly opened, and the man charged out, cigar clenched in one side of his mouth. "Bailey," he muttered by way of greeting, then thrust a stack of typed pages, covered with illegible pencil corrections, in front of Jodi. "Get off whatever you're doing and get started on these changes. We'll have more in a few minutes."

Bailey watched the stocky body in shirt sleeves disappear into his office, then shook her head. "How you can stand to work for that man is beyond me."

Jodi pushed several keys to save her document and call up another, then shrugged. "It's the old system of barter. In exchange for allowing myself to be tortured eight hours a day, I receive a paycheck that enables me to spend the other sixteen in a vain effort to recuperate. Now go away so I can concentrate on deciphering these hieroglyphics."

"You have my sympathy," Bailey called, leaving to search out Gordon and see if he had eaten lunch yet.

Bailey was working on Larry Haynes's lease the next day when Margaret called, her voice high-pitched with excitement. "Mark Powell just called to offer a settlement in the Miller case!"

"How much?"

Margaret named a sum within a thousand dollars of what Bailey had expected. Bailey leaned back in her chair and smiled at the ceiling.

"It's not enough," she told Margaret. "You need to call the client and tell her about the offer, but advise her not to take it. They'll come up with more."

"What if she wants to take it?"

"If she wants to take it, that's her decision, but as her attorney, you need to offer sound legal advice."

"Do you want to call her? I think she'd listen to you."

Obligingly Bailey returned to her office and placed the call. She wasn't surprised when Candy's initial reaction was to accept the money. However, when Bailey emphasized that the attorneys' fees would be deducted from the amount, that the first offer was always low to allow for bargaining room, and that the company would almost certainly increase their offer, she agreed to reject it.

"I'll contact opposing counsel if you'd like," Bailey offered when she called Margaret to report the outcome of her conversation with the client.

Margaret accepted gratefully.

Bailey smiled at the receiver. It would give her great pleasure to be the one to refuse Austin. Even though Mark had presented the offer, she saw no reason to go through him; Austin was obviously in charge.

However, when she called, the receptionist told her Austin was out to lunch. She left her name, then decided to go eat, also. Gordon was among the missing, too, but an educated guess told her he would likely be down the street at the deli that featured his favorite beer cheese soup on Tuesdays.

Entering the deli, she immediately spotted Gordon at a table with a large crock of soup in front of him. Seated opposite him, Austin was talking rapidly and waving his arms, his face stormy. Bailey smiled as she ordered a sandwich. She'd caught the man in a foul mood, and her news wasn't likely to improve things.

However, when Austin raised his head and saw her approaching their table, his expression lightened so noticeably, she almost lost her train of thought. He did know how to make a woman feel desirable. Damn! She shoved that idea out of her head. All he made her feel was determined, she assured herself.

"Bailey, my friend, come join us," Gordon invited.

"I just tried to call you," she said to Austin after the amenities had been observed. "I spoke with our client, and she feels the amount of your client's settlement offer is inadequate and insulting." Bailey took a satisfying bite out of her sandwich.

Austin leaned back in his chair and studied her for a minute, eyes half-closed and glittering. "It would seem," he drawled, "that you don't have much control over your client, or you'd have persuaded her to take my client's generous offer."

Bailey took her time chewing and swallowing, then leisurely sipped her iced tea, drawing out the pleasure of the encounter, of the preliminaries to winning. "On the contrary," she said, tenting her fingers beneath her chin. "My client asked my advice, and I told her we should let the jury decide. Obviously this is another case of a corporate entity trying to take advantage of the little man."

"Your client can scarcely be considered 'little.' "

"Personal insults are uncalled for."

"Perhaps, but relevant all the same." He leaned forward from his nonassertive position over the table toward Bailey. "If your client is indeed having back problems, which I doubt, I'd say she should start to solve them by joining a health club, not by trying to defraud an insurance company."

Bailey leaned forward, too, invading his space, refusing to take the defensive, though his comment about Candy, echoing her own feelings, was something of a jolt. She'd hate to think she had something in common with this arrogant, pushy man.

"I don't think discrimination against out-of-shape people is going to go over too well with a jury, since, by law of averages, several of them will be couch potatoes."

"What makes you think this case will ever get to a jury? Your client is a fraud, and our investigator will prove it."

"If that's your intent, I suggest you change investigators. The man is a total idiot. He gets drunk on the job, makes a pass at my client, can't keep his story straight."

"Our investigator would have to be a total idiot to make a pass at your client, not to mention half-blind."

The movements of Austin's lips as he spoke seemed to fill Bailey's field of vision and absorb her attention to such an extent, she had to concentrate to hear his words. She realized with a start they had both gradually risen from their chairs, and his face was only inches from hers. Her heart pounded, her breathing came shallow and rapid.

His lips had stopped moving. It was her turn to speak. She forced her gaze from his lips to his eyes. Bad move. Electrical currents leaped and sparked in those eyes, holding her as surely as if she'd grabbed a live wire.

"Poor eyesight in a detective is another valid reason for having the man disqualified," she managed to say. "Are you wearing contact lenses?" *Oh, jeez!* Why had she said that?

"What? What does that have to do with anything? My vision isn't in question."

"No, just your judgment." But the fight had gone out of her. Suddenly very aware of Austin's warm breath on her face, Bailey fell back into her chair.

He sank back, too, apparently a little confused, as well he might be. She couldn't believe she'd asked that last stupid question. Fortunately, he'd thought she was referring to his vision when she'd actually been questioning the vivid color of his eyes. She really had to keep vagrant thoughts like that out of her head or risk losing her edge.

"Where's Gordon?" Austin suddenly asked, and Bailey noticed for the first time that the chair Gordon had occupied was empty.

"Maybe he finished early," she suggested guiltily.

"His bowl and glass are gone," Austin observed.

A quick scan of the small room revealed Gordon sitting a couple of tables away. Upon being discovered, he smiled and waved. Bailey motioned for him to return, and he sauntered over.

"Is it safe?" he asked, resuming his seat.

"Gordon, how can you possibly expect to be a successful lawyer when you can't stand a little controversy?" she asked him.

"Simple, my dear. I don't. In years to come, I'll probably set a record as the oldest associate at Hoskins, Grier, as well as the lawyer with the fewest ulcers."

Bailey shook her head fondly. "You're hopeless."

"Unless, of course," Gordon continued, "management should change at the old place and someone come in with streamlined, efficient ideas."

"Then what would you do?" Austin asked, sounding suddenly solemn.

"I don't know. Travel, maybe. Write a book. Paint."

"Not likely since the terms of your trust fund require you to practice law." Austin's gaze never left Gordon's face, and Bailey wondered if he knew something she didn't.

"You're such a stickler for facts! Okay, I'd open my own firm and hire you two enthusiasts to carry the work load while I play." He rattled the ice in his plastic tumbler, tossed a piece into his mouth, and crunched. "Or maybe I'll discover the ever elusive reason for working and then become a better lawyer than you two put together. That is to say, a more successful lawyer, not a more aggressive one, since that would not only be undesirable but impossible.''

What a strange thing for him to say, Bailey thought. Why would he call her aggressive?

FOUR

As Austin walked back to his office after lunch, he found that a smile kept sneaking onto his face for no reason. He hadn't won the argument with Bailey, though he hadn't lost either. Still, he should be upset because she had rejected the settlement offer. In all honesty, though, he had to admit he'd known she would. She was tough, a worthy adversary. Battling with her certainly got his adrenaline pumping, not to mention the decided effect she had on his hormones.

Inside the building, he punched the button to call the elevator, and his smile slowly dwindled. He had to meet with Daniel Lewis, and that wouldn't be nearly as much fun as sparring with Bailey.

A few minutes later, Austin entered the corner office and faced the older man. Even seated behind the desk, Lewis was obviously tall. Of course, some of that was probably an optical illusion created by his gauntness and long, drooping facial features. He reminded Austin of a skinny basset hound, but his tenacity was that of a bulldog.

"Have you started negotiations with Stafford Morris yet?" Austin asked without preamble, taking a seat without invitation. Though Lewis was third in overall seniority in the firm, he had been managing partner of the Kansas City branch for fifteen years, and Austin knew he resented this intrusion into what he considered his territory.

"I've talked to Stafford."

Probably about where to go for lunch, Austin thought wryly. "And what was his feeling about a merger?"

"Negotiations take time."

Austin's fingers drummed silently on the padded arm of the chair. "As we discussed before, perhaps I should help with the negotiations since you and Stafford are friends."

"I've been doing business with Stafford Morris for a lot of years—" He stopped speaking, but the inflection of his voice didn't go down, clearly leaving the sentence unfinished. Austin could complete it in his mind—"without your help."

"Tell you what. Why don't you arrange a meeting to include me, just as an observer? Shall we say next week?"

"I'll see what I can do."

That meant about a fifty-fifty chance.

"Fine. Don't forget our meetings with public relations firms on Tuesday and Friday."

With a vague nod, Lewis turned his attention back to the papers on his desk, dismissing Austin. As he left the office, he heard the older man mutter, "Public relations for lawyers. Humph!"

Returning to the tiny cubicle he was using as a temporary office, Austin flopped into the creaky chair and made an effort to unclench his teeth. Damn it, he'd been chosen for this job because of his proven abilities. But these people were fighting him at every turn, making him prove everything all over again.

Picking up a pencil, he tapped the eraser end on the scarred desktop. Well, if he had to, he would, starting with this merger. The firm had approved the merger by majority vote. Now it was his job to see that the deal was consummated.

However, while the idea of taking in Stafford Morris' group had its merits, he'd recently come to realize there could be a problem. The pencil snapped in his fingers. What about Gordon? Kearns, Worley expected all their employees to maintain a consistently high level of productivity. Somehow he'd have to protect Gordon, or make him work harder.

He tossed the broken pencil into the trash. Protecting him would probably be the easier way to go.

"Can't do lunch today," Gordon advised Bailey on Friday when she called him. "I'm taking Jodi over to the newspaper office to pick up her replies to her personal ad so she won't have to wait for them to be mailed."

"Good thinking," Bailey responded. "If she gets any, take them away from her and burn them."

"Mm, well, got to run. Okay if I come by tonight?"

"Of course. You know where the spare key is if I'm not there. Some of us have to work."

"Jodi'll be there," he reminded her.

Bailey breathed a sign of relief as she hung up the phone. Good old Gordon. He'd see that Jodi didn't get involved with any nuts as a result of her impetuous ad.

When she finally made it home after an extra hard, long day, she found the two of them on the white sofa in her living room, reading, discussing, and grading Jodi's replies.

"That one is a definite 'No Way,' " Gordon advised as Jodi's hand hovered uncertainly over the three stacks of letters on Bailey's glass and brass coffee table.

"I don't know," Jodi demurred. "Sipping wine before the fireplace, walking in the rain—he sounds kind of sweet. I think the 'Maybe' stack."

"You're both nuts!" Bailey exclaimed, picking up Samantha and heading for the kitchen. "All those letters belong in your 'No Way' stack. Sipping wine and walking in the rain—they're probably all wet, drunk mass murderers, and married besides." She scowled over the pass-through bar from the kitchen into the living room. "And you, Gordon! I can't believe you're aiding and abetting this insanity."

"Ignore her," Jodi said, dropping the letter in her middle stack.

"I usually do," Gordon drawled.

"I suppose you'd rather I went to a bar to meet somebody." Ripping open a cream-colored envelope, Jodi raised an eyebrow in Bailey's direction.

"I'd rather you joined a nunnery," she retorted. "Go back to school. That's where you met your exhusband."

"Right. In grade school."

Unable to argue with that, Bailey turned her attention to scooping dog food into a royal blue bowl with SA-MANTHA in white letters. "Come see what I cooked for your dinner, sweetheart," she said, placing the bowl on the white kitchen tile.

The dog pranced over, sniffed, then looked at Bailey with an aggrieved expression.

"Okay, so it's only dog food out of a can. You ought to be glad. What if you actually had to eat my cooking?"

"Hey, listen to this," Jodi called.

Bailey scratched Samantha's head and, leaving her to her repast, crossed the blue carpet to join Jodi.

" 'Dear Cinderella,' " Jodi read from the ivory paper. " 'My faithful servant brought me the copy of your note, and I hastened to reply lest you be overwhelmed by an army of unreasonable facsimiles. For, of course, I am the only real Prince Charming. Actually, I'm king now since my father retired and moved to Texas, but King Charming doesn't have quite the same ring, does it?

" 'Since the post office system is so mundane and

totally unsuitable for use by such as we, may I suggest we maintain further contact via the secret royal chamber for missives. If you go to the park named Regency and travel twenty paces from the northeast corner of the rose garden, then turn and go twelve paces to your left, you will come upon a large tree. There you'll find said chamber cleverly disguised as a hole beneath the roots. Do respond soon as I shan't be able to attend to the duties of the kingdom until I hear from you. Faithfully, PC.' "

"You have to make a new stack for that one," Gordon declared. " 'Definitely at Once.' "

"Absolutely," Jodi agreed. "The kingdom might be besieged and lost, all because I didn't answer the man."

"You're going to write a letter to that lunatic?" Bailey asked in amazement.

"At least he's a romantic lunatic." Jodi stood and raised her head haughtily. "Come along, Gordon. We'll find my typewriter and compose a suitable reply."

Gordon stood and took Jodi's arm to escort her from the room. "A typewriter sounds sort of mundane. Do you think maybe this letter should be handwritten on perfumed stationery?"

"Nah. My handwriting is totally illegible. It's why I had to learn to type. Anyway, PC typed his letter."

"Dictated it to the court stenographer, probably."

The pair went into gales of laughter as they disappeared into Jodi's room.

Bailey reached down and scooped up Samantha as the little dog strolled into the room. "I do believe you're the only sane friend I have," she told her.

Samantha snuggled in, twisting and turning before finally settling with a contented sigh in a fuzzy ball in Bailey's lap. Bailey stroked the soft fur and wondered why she didn't feel content. Usually Friday nights left her with a sense of accomplishment and an anticipation of the weekend. Saturday work was leisurely compared to the rest of the week, so Friday evening started a time of relaxation, but tonight she felt unsettled.

"Want to go get something to eat?" she called to her demented friends.

"How about we send out for a pizza?" Jodi asked.

"Sounds good to me," Gordon seconded.

Resignedly Bailey reached for the phone, wondering if they planned to come out of the bedroom to eat. Just as her hand touched the instrument, however, it rang.

Her lack of surprise at hearing Austin's voice gave her a moment's pause, but she assured herself it was only because they'd talked at least once a day concerning the Miller case during the past week. Expecting his voice was a normal response, not a psychic link or anything weird.

"Yes, Gordon's here," she replied in response to his query. "At least, his body is. He's totally lost his mind." She explained what Gordon and Jodi were doing, expecting a sympathetic ear.

"They're *both* writing a letter to Prince Charming?" Austin asked, the emphasis indicating it would be okay if only one of them were doing the writing.

"Hang on. I'll get your friend for you," Bailey offered. Apparently Austin wasn't going to be an ally—was, in fact, involved in the nuttiness.

Gordon's first response to Austin was laughter, then a cryptic "Guidance could be critical."

The entire conversation sounded suspicious to Bailey—Gordon's tone as well as his avoidance of coherent statements.

"See if he wants to come over for pizza," she invited. Best to find out what the two of them were up to, she told herself, justifying the action.

"He says he'll even bring the pizza," Gordon informed her.

An hour later Austin arrived with cold beer and hot pizza. Bailey directed him to the refrigerator while she set the cardboard box in the middle of her dining room table.

"I'm surprised you have a table," Austin said, coming up behind her, leaning over her shoulder to peer at the polished wood with glass inserts. "I mean, since you don't have anything in the refrigerator except dog food and mayonnaise."

"I keep sodas in the vegetable bins," she snapped, suddenly acutely aware of his closeness, afraid to move for fear she'd touch him, uncertain and fearful of where that touch might take her.

For a moment they stood, a tense tableau, then Gordon and Jodi burst into the room. Austin stepped backward, and Bailey darted into the kitchen for plates.

"Austin, you wouldn't believe how many replies I've already got to my ad," Jodi announced. "Here, listen to this one."

Jodi read her letter from Prince Charming while the others consumed pizza. Taking a huge bite of her piece, she chewed a couple of times, then declared, "And now you have to hear this really incredible letter Gordon and I have composed in answer."

"No!" both men objected at once.

"Why not?"

"That's very personal, Jodi," Austin replied. "I think you should keep the contents strictly between you and this—this PC."

Bailey studied Austin's face as he spoke. Something about this deal wasn't on the up and up.

When the last piece of pizza had been consumed, Austin and Gordon settled comfortably in the living room chairs facing Bailey and Jodi on the sofa. Bailey felt satiated, relaxed, and surprisingly comfortable in spite of Austin's presence.

"So how do you like working for the old bear?" Austin asked Jodi.

Jodi looked at him, then turned away as Samantha bounced into her lap. "It's a job," she answered, shrugging, stroking the dog as she again raised her eyes to Austin. "The only one I'm qualified for at this stage of my life."

With a start Bailey realized that Jodi really did hate being a legal secretary as much as she said she did. Since she tended to be sarcastic about most things, Bailey had mostly dismissed her comments. But Jodi's lilting voice had suddenly gone dull and lifeless.

"So why don't you do something else?" Bailey asked.

"Like what? I'm too short to be a model and too clumsy to be a waitress. And speaking of, what's happening with our friend Candy?"

"Don't get them started," Gordon warned. "We'll have World War Three right here in Bailey's living room. Come on, let's go deliver your letter."

"Right now? In the middle of the night?"

"Sure." He stood, pulling Jodi to her feet. "Why not? I'll protect you."

"It's not that," she answered. "It just doesn't feel right to send off a letter without making file and reading copies."

"You've definitely been a secretary too long. Come on."

Jodi retrieved the envelope from the kitchen bar, sealed it, and grinned. "This is fun," she said.

"We'll be back shortly," Gordon assured Bailey and Austin as he opened the door for Jodi.

"You know, we can't stretch you or improve your coordination, but have you ever considered night school now that you live close to several colleges?" Gordon asked her.

Bailey watched the pair leave, the door close behind them. Even if they were nuts, she was glad her two best friends got along so well. She didn't even resent their going off together and leaving her alone with Austin. But suddenly she didn't feel so comfortable anymore.

Ridiculous! She'd overcome this irrational fear of the male of the species long ago. She was a professional, a skilled attorney up for a partnership. So why did Austin make her feel like she was sixteen again?

For what seemed an eternity but was probably only a few seconds, she kept her head turned toward the door, avoiding him, searching her usually fertile mind for something to say. They'd argued interminably all week, creating an odd sort of intimacy by virtue of the continued encounters. There was really no reason to feel awkward now.

With incredible force for a six-pound creature, Samantha leaped into Bailey's lap, eliciting a startled "Oomph!"

"Cute dog," Austin said, and she finally turned to look at him, directly into those electric eyes.

"Thanks," she said, her voice barely above a whisper.

A mantel clock that had heretofore been relatively silent now ticked loudly, annoyingly.

"Nice chess set," Austin said. The carved ivory figures on a marble board occupied their own table in the corner of the room.

"A gift from my father. Do you play?"

"A little." But his eyes lit up, and Bailey knew.

Wordlessly she moved the set to the dining room table, and Austin followed, eyes glowing. As they began to play, she rapidly concluded that he was no novice. Not that she'd ever thought he might be.

Bailey's blood was leaping again. She made her moves unhesitatingly, no longer uncomfortable, again in control.

Sometime during the game she saw Jodi and Gordon from the corner of her eye as they came in, but they went straight to Jodi's room.

Finally—

"Check," Austin announced.

"And mate." Bailey unhesitatingly moved a knight into position, trying to refrain from smirking.

"Very good," Austin said. *Damn!* he thought. That gave her two in a row, for she'd definitely trounced him at the deposition. "Another game?" He had her strategies figured out now. He'd beat her this time.

Some time later he slapped his palm on the tabletop and exclaimed, "Impossible!" when it became apparent the game was a stalemate.

"My sentiments exactly."

For a moment they glared at each other, then both shoved back their chairs and stood. Austin moved in long strides toward the refrigerator. From the corner of his eye, he saw Bailey doing the same thing. Well, he could certainly walk faster than she could!

They collided in the kitchen doorway. He automatically put up his hands to brace against the collision, and she must have done the same, because somehow their bodies slammed together while their arms tangled around each other. The adrenaline of anger, the excitement of the game, somehow all got mixed up and misdirected. He could have sworn it all came from holding Bailey's sleek body against his.

Her face, inches from his own, was glowing, her green eyes blazing. She exuded life and vitality and challenge.

One of his hands, seemingly of its own volition, stroked her smooth neck while the other moved down her slim waist.

This is crazy, he thought. Holding an untamed tiger in one's arms is definitely crazy, but it didn't feel crazy. It felt wonderful.

He really had to stop.

Her full lips parted slightly, as if to take in extra breaths, her gaze never leaving his. Her hands caressed his back, deftly, gently, as he'd never realized—had always known—she could.

Austin ordered his hands to move away from her

body, but they were no longer connected to his brain. The one slid down to the firm roundness of her buttocks, pushed her pelvis against his arousal, while the other held her neck firmly as his lips touched hers. She returned the kiss hungrily, matching his own frenzy. He felt the strength and the softness, tasted pizza and beer and an elusive spiciness he immediately identified as Bailey. His tongue darted out, met hers, thrust, parried, retreated, and returned.

He couldn't think, didn't dare think, could only revel in the feel of her beneath his hands, against his body, moving with him in a frenetic rhythm. As she clung to him, his hands moved from her neck, over her collarbone, down to her small, round breast, molding it through the soft fabric of her cotton blouse. His fingers searched for the nipple, his breath coming faster as he found it erect, felt her surge against him as he stroked.

Something gentle but insistent touched his leg repeatedly, but he had no attention left for outside distractions. This contest was consuming him. He couldn't get enough of Bailey. He had to have her, had to love her, doubted even that would be enough.

A sharp bark intruded.

Dazed, Austin jerked apart from Bailey, followed her gaze to the floor at their feet where Samantha looked up with indignation in her brown eyes.

Bailey sank to the floor, took the dog into her arms. "Were you being ignored, sweetheart?" Her words were gasps, the same as his would be if he tried to talk.

Talk? How could he talk when he couldn't even think? Austin yanked open the refrigerator door and pulled out a can of beer. He popped the top, held on to the kitchen counter, and downed half the contents of the can, then paused to breathe.

"Are you two finally taking a break?" Jodi's voice came across the room.

"Yes," he gulped.

"We're finished," Bailey added.

She sounded so definite, but when he looked at her, in the split second before she looked away, he saw in her eyes what he already knew. They weren't. They'd barely begun, and whatever it was they'd begun, it was like nothing he'd ever known or heard of before.

"Got to run, kids," Gordon said, giving Jodi and Bailey a quick kiss. "Let's do my place tomorrow night. Austin and I will cook so we can eat something besides pizza."

Austin smiled as he felt control returning. He was a gourmet cook. No woman who kept dog food and mayonnaise in her refrigerator could possibly equal his culinary skills. "Great idea, Gordon."

FIVE

Bailey set her grocery sacks on the kitchen counter, then went back downstairs for her large shopping bag from The Complete Kitchen. Who'd have thought a little cheesecake would require so many different items? But it would be worth all the hassle to see the look on Austin's face when she brought a white chocolate cheesecake with raspberry sauce for dessert.

With the various bags settled on the counter, she reached down to scoop up Samantha.

"Your uncle Gordon's going to get his, too," she told the little dog. "Imagine, telling me which kind of frozen cheesecake he liked best when I offered to bring dessert."

"Bailey, you're home early," Jodi exclaimed.

Bailey started at the sound of her friend's voice. Jodi entered the living room with a fist full of letters.

"Why aren't you out at the pool trying to catch skin cancer?" she asked, hoping Jodi wouldn't look in the kitchen.

"You're just jealous because you look like a speckled pup after a few minutes in the sun. What have you got in the sacks?"

Bailey tilted her chin upward. "I'm taking dessert to Gordon's tonight."

"That's a lot of dessert. What did you do? Buy out all the Pepperidge Farm cookies?" Jodi came over to peek into the bags.

"I'm *making* dessert. That's the ingredients and a pan and measuring stuff and a cookbook. Now go lie in the sun or stuff your letters in a tree or something."

"Good grief! It really is." She lifted out a springform pan and set of measuring cups. "Bailey, dear friend, I feel it's my duty to remind you that you can't cook. Have you forgotten being the only person in the history of Haywood High who did a supplemental research paper so you wouldn't flunk home ec?"

"Any idiot can cook. It's like a computer program. You just follow the directions."

Jodi pulled a package of white chocolate from one of the bags and studied it appraisingly. "I can mail my letters later. I don't think I'd better leave right now."

"Jodi Lynn Duvall, don't you touch one thing in this kitchen. *I'm* cooking, and I don't need any criticism or help."

"You don't mind if I sit here at the bar and drink iced tea, do you?"

Most assuredly Bailey minded, but there seemed no way out of it. "Fine. But knock off the unsolicited advice."

"I'll just sit here quiet as a mouse and take notes. Maybe we could work this into a television sitcom."

Choosing to ignore her friend's smart mouth, Bailey left the room to change into appropriate attire.

Minutes later, wearing the T-shirt and shorts she'd worn to paint the bedroom, Bailey unpacked her purchases and arranged them on the counter. She studied the recipe carefully, then rearranged everything and stared at the items, trying vainly to imagine the gorgeous color picture in the cookbook emerging from all that mess. Jodi had her head buried in a magazine, but Bailey could have sworn she was smirking.

Taking a deep breath, she turned her attention to the project. One thing she knew for certain—the blasted recipe had to be followed exactly. Jodi's recounting of her high school fiasco, her last experiment with cooking, reminded her that cutting out unnecessary steps had gotten her in trouble before.

She set the oven to the exact temperature, allowing time for it to preheat, then consulted the recipe again. Since she didn't have time to let the cream cheese reach room temperature while lying on the counter, she plopped it into the microwave, where parts of it got real soft real fast. Well, it could harden up a little in the freezer while she made the crust.

Finally, after what seemed an eternity, the cheesecake was in the oven. Now to get all the seeds out of those raspberries and make the sauce. Maybe if she just put them in the blender, the seeds would mush up and disappear.

Yes, indeed, Austin would regret his tacky remarks about her refrigerator holding nothing but dog food and mayonnaise. She'd show him she was a skilled cook.

"This is great," Gordon drawled, popping the tab on a beer and settling onto a dining table chair.

"You get to clean up," Austin answered from the kitchen, stuffing wild rice mixture into the last Cornish game hen.

"You're such a pal, going to so much trouble to help me impress Jodi."

Austin hesitated in his work, searching for sarcasm in Gordon's words. "Seems to me you need all the help you can get," he finally said. "What you're doing is the goofiest thing I've ever heard of. Where do you go from here? You can't leave letters in the park indefinitely." He basted the birds carefully with real butter. This was no time to think of one's arteries.

"I'm glad you asked. I've got a great idea, and since you're so eager to help, I'll include you. I take her to the park to look for her next letter, and I let you know when we're going. Then you be there waiting, and while we go check the tree, you leave flowers in her car."

Austin slid the hens into the oven and groaned. He'd never known his friend to go to so much trouble over a woman—over anything, for that matter. If a project involved effort, Gordon just left it and went on to something easier.

"Has it ever occurred to you that when Jodi finds out you're writing these kooky letters, she may just decide you're nuts in addition to being a lawyer? Then she'll for sure never go out with you. Probably never speak to you again."

"I'm just trying to give her a chance to see what kind of guy I am without being blinded by her prejudice against lawyers."

Austin joined his friend on the brown leather sofa. "I'm beginning to think she may be right about attorneys."

"They're still ready to lynch you, huh?"

"They're fighting the changes." Austin noticed a small spot of butter on his crisply creased khaki slacks. He considered going home to change, then discarded the idea. If he did that, Gordon might think he was unduly concerned about how he looked tonight, might think he was trying to impress Bailey. He crossed his leg over the spot. "They're stodgy," he finished, coming back to the subject at hand.

"They've done pretty good for a lot of years." Gordon leaned back, swung his legs onto the sturdy coffee table.

"But the world has changed, the practice of law has changed. If we don't change, too, we'll be swallowed up by progressive firms that do. We have to streamline our work habits, cut out waste, and, of course, get a good public relations firm.''

"Austin, are you sure you were sent over here because you did so well with the St. Louis office, or because they wanted to get rid of you?''

"You've been hanging around your friend Bailey too long. Her abrasive personality's rubbing off.'' He had to do that, had to say Bailey's name aloud, as if he could thus summon her up.

Gordon smiled lazily. "Old friend, if *your* abrasive personality didn't rub off on me over the years, I don't think I'm in any danger from Bailey. You, on the other hand . . .'' Gordon shrugged, drained his beer can, and crushed it.

"Me on the other hand what?'' Austin sat forward, studying his friend's face closely.

"Have met your match, I'd say. I'm going to hit the shower and get all spiffed up.'' He stood, stretched, and looked back at Austin. "Like you. And if you keep your legs crossed, Bailey will never see that spot of butter.'' He strolled from the room.

Well, Austin thought, staring after his friend, either the man was awfully perceptive or he had observed the spectacle of the night before. Austin couldn't quite decide if that bothered him or not; but then, he couldn't quite decide what to make of that kiss, either. One thing he was sure of, though; he had to take exception to Gordon's assertion that he'd "met his match.'' She could certainly put the pressure on him, force him to give his very best, but he'd still be the ultimate winner.

True, she was mentally acute and physically trim, athletic, without an ounce of fat on her slim body. Even her rounded derrière was firm. Though, he recalled with pleasure, her breast had been soft and pliant beneath his hand, only the nipple swelling hard between his fingers.

Damn! How did he get off on that line of thought?

e forced the smile off his face before Gordon came
back in and noticed.

Austin was in the kitchen putting the finishing
touches on his Caesar salad when Bailey and Jodi
arrived.

"That looks wonderful," he heard Gordon enthuse.
"Where did you get it? A new bakery?"

"I made it." Bailey's voice rang with indignant
defiance.

Gordon laughed, but Jodi interrupted. "She did. I
watched. It's kind of scary, really."

Gordon had told him she was insistent about bringing
something, but it would probably be frozen.

He leaned into the living room, eager to see what
she'd come up with. Jodi, cute and perky in a denim
miniskirt, held Samantha in her arms. Gordon looked
amused. Bailey, striding regally, carried a cut-glass
cake plate holding an incredible culinary creation.

"White chocolate cheesecake with raspberry sauce,"
she announced, handing it to him. "Just something I
whipped up on the spur of the moment."

Austin accepted the plate but continued to stare at
Bailey. In a flowing cotton skirt patterned with flowers;
and a pale green blouse that accented her flushed cheeks
and sparkling ocean eyes, she looked willowy, ethe-
real—his mind groped for the right words—beautiful,
female, desirable.

"You made this?" he finally managed to ask, diverting his thoughts before they got too carried away.

For an instant her eyes blazed with indignant green
fire at his rude question, but her reply was cool.
"Umm-hmm," she said, and turned her back to him.
"Gordon, is that a new painting?"

Later, as they finished dinner, Bailey had to admit
the meal was wonderful, even if Austin had cooked it.
Of course, her cheesecake would be every bit as won-

derful. Magnanimously she added her praise to the compliments of Gordon and Jodi.

"It's just something I whipped up on the spur of the moment," he replied, mocking her earlier comment.

Okay, that was fair, Bailey decided. "Touché," she said. "Actually, I spent more time and effort on that blasted cheesecake than I spend preparing a case for trial."

"Half that effort was expended in cursing," Jodi explained, and everyone laughed.

Bailey felt mellow, warm in the company of friends, even Austin. Eagerly she anticipated his approval of her creation—grudging approval, probably. He'd hate to admit she'd won again. Grudging but respectful. Yes, she liked that idea.

"How about we adjourn to the living room?" Gordon suggested. "Is everybody up to real coffee with dessert, or should I make decaf? Bailey, would you come slice your cheesecake?"

When everyone was settled with a steaming cup of coffee, Bailey proudly served pieces of the cream-colored dessert, topped by bright red splashes. Gordon and Jodi murmured compliments as they prepared to take their first bite. Austin was silent, but that was to be expected. Naturally he'd resent her stealing his thunder.

She watched them as they chewed and swallowed, waited for expressions of delight. No one said anything, nor did they take a second bite.

"Well?" she finally asked when they all seemed intent on draining their coffee cups.

Gordon set his dish on the coffee table. Samantha prissed over, sniffed, turned up her nose, and walked away. The three of them burst into laughter.

"Did you do this on purpose?" Gordon asked.

"Bailey, dear friend, I think you'd better stick to being a lawyer," Jodi suggested.

"You're all very funny," Bailey retorted, taking her own first bite.

Maybe they weren't just being funny. It didn't taste quite right. In fact, it tasted pretty awful, sort of like greasy cardboard with gritty raspberries. But her difficulty in swallowing wasn't just from the bad flavor. A big lump seemed to have risen in her throat.

As if that weren't bad enough, she looked up to find Austin staring directly at her, those unnatural eyes piercing to her very soul. She wanted to run home and hide for the rest of her life.

In the distance, far away, she could hear Jodi telling the home ec story. The floor didn't seem likely to open up beneath her feet, so she'd have to face the situation head-on.

Then Austin's voice cut through the fog, loud and clear. "My compliments," he said smoothly, actually forking another bite into his mouth.

Bailey watched him in stunned fascination.

"Austin, you're going to die a painful death," Gordon warned.

"Gordon, remember how I used to tell you your taste was all in your mouth? Well, I take that back. It certainly isn't there, either, if you can't appreciate the delicate flavor of this dessert. You've become accustomed to the frozen variety. This is unique, homemade, more like the deli varieties in New York." So saying, he took another bite.

The overblown praise had to be sarcasm. Yet he continued to eat and smile.

Doubting her own judgment, Bailey took another bite, searching for the New York flavor. This bite went down easier because the lump in her throat was dissolving, but it didn't taste any better. If that was what they liked in New York, she'd continue to take her vacations in the South.

Looking up, she caught Jodi and Gordon exchanging confused glances, then retrieving their plates for another taste. Puzzled, she turned her attention to Austin, but he was concentrating on eating and didn't look up.

This made no sense. He couldn't possibly like greasy cardboard. If it were anyone but Austin, she'd think he was being kind, trying to make her feel good, throwing the race.

Somehow she made it through the rest of the evening, but she didn't dare look at Austin. If she'd seen sympathy or pity in his eyes, she couldn't have stood it. That would be the ultimate sign of losing.

Finally it was time to leave, to get away from everyone, to hide, regain control, and sort out the evening.

"Did you check the park today?" Gordon asked Jodi as Bailey unlocked the car doors and plopped Samantha into the backseat.

"No. I'm going tomorrow. Which reminds me . . ." She opened the passenger door and retrieved Bailey's ill-fated shopping bag from The Complete Kitchen. "I answered twenty of the letters from prospective Prince Charmings." She turned to Bailey. "We need to mail them on the way home."

"Austin'll do it," Gordon exclaimed, stepping quickly to the car, taking the bag from Jodi, and passing it to Austin. "He has to go right by a post office on his way home. You don't need to be stopping this late at night."

"Okay," Jodi agreed, shrugging. "About time you lawyers did some of the mailing."

"Pick you up tomorrow to go to the park," Gordon called as they pulled away from the curb. Jodi leaned out the window to wave.

"You know," she said, rolling up the window, "it's a shame those guys are lawyers."

"Umm," Bailey murmured noncommittally, refusing to relinquish her train of thought. She'd found something to take her mind off the evening's events, and she didn't want to give it up. What did they want with

Jodi's letters, and why did Gordon want to take her to the park?

"They were both so gallant tonight. Especially Austin. Kind of surprising, considering the way you two fight, but I suppose that makes it all the more chivalrous."

"What do you mean?" Bailey gripped the steering wheel.

"Austin saving your honor, of course."

"Saving my honor?" Somehow that had a nicer ring than feeling sorry for her.

"Sure, by eating that horrible cheesecake. You're lucky you make enough money to eat out all the time, because you really are the worst cook I've ever known."

"Maybe he liked it," Bailey protested. *Saving my honor?* She fought against the disconcerting warm spot the idea planted in the middle of her chest.

"No way. He just didn't realize that you know you're a lousy cook, and that it doesn't bother you. Still, he was a real gentlemen to come to your defense."

"My defense? I don't need anyone to defend me! Certainly not Austin Travers!"

"Well, you must admit, he had the perfect opportunity to roast you, and he didn't do it. Maybe he suddenly noticed you're a woman. You do look really good tonight."

Bailey was grateful for the darkness in the car. She could feel the blood rushing to her face as Jodi's words reminded her of the way she'd felt in Austin's arms only last night, of the kiss they'd shared. Though calling it a kiss was like calling Niagara Falls a creek. And tonight he'd "saved her honor."

Austin slouched low in the seat of his Mercedes, waiting for Jodi and Gordon to arrive. Sitting in the park with a huge basket of cut flowers in the passenger seat, trying to be unobtrusive, was ridiculous. Stealing Jodi's letters rather than mailing them was bad enough, but this escapade was worse.

He shifted and scanned the parking lot carefully, anxious to spot Gordon's familiar car and get it over with. Gordon would really owe him after cooking that dinner last night and delivering flowers anonymously today. Of course—he cringed—Gordon might think he'd paid his dues by being forced into eating more of that awful cheesecake.

And there was another piece of insanity. He'd had Bailey on the mat, beaten her fair and square. His cooking was delicious, and hers was terrible. Yet he'd thrown the race.

Her expression when she'd taken her first bite flashed onto his brain—those big, clear eyes so full of despair. Logically he knew he should have jumped on her when she was down, since that seemed to be about the only time he *could* jump on her. He should have refused to eat the blasted cheesecake, should have added his insults to the others.

He should have jumped out of his chair and pulled her to her feet and kissed those sad lips. He should have taken them both back to that crazy world they'd found on Friday night.

Kiss her or fight her. There seemed to be no middle ground.

He slammed out of the car and walked across the parking lot, onto the grass, not caring if Jodi saw him.

Fresh air, that was the ticket. Get his head clear.

As soon as this was over, he'd go to the club and work out. Better yet, he'd go for a long run. There was another 10-K coming up in a couple of weeks, and he had to be ready to trounce Bailey soundly when that time came. His lips curved in an involuntary smile at the thought, and the tension left his body. He'd finish, he decided, half a mile in front of her.

Hands in his pockets, he strolled back toward his

car, admiring the roses, breathing in their aroma, noticing for the first time how blue the sky was. He almost didn't see Gordon and Jodi as they drove up. With a sigh, he backed around a tree, hoping no one he knew would see such strange behavior.

Jodi was talking a mile a minute, and Gordon was beaming down on her. Gads! He certainly hoped he never became that besotted with a woman.

As soon as they were out of sight, he retrieved the flowers from his car, set them in the front seat of Gordon's, and ran back to his own. Thank goodness that was over!

Opening the sunroof, he turned the radio up and pulled away, singing along. He'd call Bailey and invite her to run with him this evening.

Across the lot, Bailey's lips narrowed as she watched the scenario unfold. She'd known all along that something was screwy about this whole PC business. Following Jodi and Gordon to the park had seemed a little silly, but she had been determined to find out what was going on.

Now it all made sense. She should have figured it out before. Gordon pushing Jodi about this Prince Charming thing, making sure she made it to the park, Austin always hanging around, being "gallant" and "chivalrous," Austin volunteering to mail Jodi's letters. She'd be willing to bet those letters never made it to the post office.

Her heart shriveled. Painful as it was, she had to admit that she'd come to think of Austin as "hers." Maybe not in the standard sense, but hers to fight with and run with and maybe even kiss again. He'd eaten her cheesecake and stood with her against Jodi and Gordon. But in the end, it was Jodi he'd been coming to see—petite, pretty Jodi.

Who was it who said, "The more things change, the more they stay the same"? Gangly, awkward Bailey, with braces and freckles, had let the boys copy her homework, but Jodi had been the one who went to proms.

She twisted the key and gunned the engine, screeching out of the parking lot.

SIX

Back in her bedroom, Bailey cursed softly, then more loudly as the zipper of her black skirt jammed and refused to budge. Of all times—she wanted to be dressed and gone when Jodi and Gordon came back. She almost wished she'd gone on to the office in her cutoffs. Everyone else dressed casually on weekends. Only she felt office attire was appropriate when in the office, no matter the day or hour, and today it was proving to be her undoing.

She didn't want to see her friends, to be forced to act as if everything was all right, her life was neat and orderly, the way it had always been. None of the above was true, and she didn't have the emotional energy to pretend it was.

Well, that's what she got for trying to compete in an area in which she had inadequate training and skills.

A gentle touch on her leg turned her attention to Samantha. The little dog was looking up with liquid, pleading eyes. She knew that stockings and suits meant her friend was going away. Bailey reached down and picked her up, balancing the furry body in one hand and scratching her ears with the other.

"You can go with me, sweetheart. On Sundays the

81

office belongs to us. You can lie right in the middle of Stafford Morris' desk if you like. Dig yourself a nice bed in his papers. Just don't get in the ashtray. You'd never be clean again."

Samantha twisted and scrambled onto Bailey's shoulder, snuggling comfortably against her neck.

"Sometimes, little one, I think you know more than you let on," Bailey murmured, stroking the soft fur. She couldn't be totally dejected around so much love.

From the living room came the sound of a door closing, followed by Jodi's bubbling laughter. Plopping Samantha onto her white bedspread, Bailey gave the zipper a final yank and felt it jerk free. She threw on her jacket, grabbed her black leather shoulder bag and Samantha, and strode out of her bedroom.

Gordon was positioning the telltale flower arrangement in the middle of the coffee table. Samantha squirmed from Bailey's grasp and ran over to greet Jodi, then Gordon, then Jodi again.

"Bailey," Jodi called, seating herself on the sofa directly in front of the flowers and next to Gordon. "Come look. While Gordon and I went to retrieve my latest letter, Prince Charming left these in my car. Isn't that romantic?"

"They're lovely flowers."

Bailey tried to keep her voice neutral, but Jodi's eyes narrowed as she turned her full attention to Bailey. "Why are you dressed like that?" she asked.

"I'm going to a costume party as a lawyer. Why do you think I'm dressed like this? I'm going down to the office for a while."

"It's Sunday afternoon," Gordon protested. "Jodi and I were talking about maybe calling Austin, and we could all go down to that park over by my house for the free concert. Take a blanket and some cheap wine and pretend we're in college again."

"I never went to college," Jodi reminded him.

"Yeah, but you've got a great imagination."

They both laughed giddily at the stupid remarks. Bailey felt relief when the telephone shrilled its interruption. She rushed to answer it, to get away from the conversation that centered around Jodi and Austin.

"Bailey," Austin's voice boomed over the wire. So much for feeling relief.

In an instant she considered and rejected a multitude of responses ranging from "What do you want?" to "Go to hell."

"Yes?" was the best she could come up with.

Should she ask if he wanted to talk to Jodi, make it easier for him? Hell, no, she decided.

"Have you registered for that 10-K race on Saturday after next?" he asked.

"Not yet." And she wouldn't if he was going to be there.

"I thought you might like to get in a practice run," he went on, seemingly oblivious to her curt reply. "It's a great afternoon for running—low humidity, starting to cool a little. In an hour or so it'll be perfect. We could even wait until evening. I love to run after dark, don't you?"

She did, but she wasn't going to admit it to him. "It's dangerous to run after dark in the city."

Austin's laughter roared in her ear. "Bailey, I feel deeply sorry for anyone who tries to attack you. Anyway, I'll be running with you. A little ahead, probably, but still within earshot. Why don't we get Gordon and Jodi, grab a light, early dinner, then you and I can go for a late run?"

Obviously he and Gordon needed to get together on their stories. "Gordon wants to go to the free concert in the park."

"Sounds good to me. We can let our dinner settle while we listen to a couple of songs, then go for a run, come back, and listen some more."

Yeah, and you can . . . Bailey thought, then stopped herself. So she hated Austin and was jealous of Jodi.

So Jodi hated lawyers, and she herself thought a relationship between the two would be disastrous for Jodi.
That wasn't really her decision to make. If using her
was the only way he could get close to Jodi, she should
just go along with it and let Jodi decide. However . . .

"Blow it out your ear," she said, and hung up the
phone.

"Was that, by any chance, Austin?" Gordon asked.

"Umm. Excuse me. I really have to get to the office." She leaned over, clapped her hands, and Samantha jumped into her arms.

"Bailey!" Jodi swung over the back of the sofa in
front of her. "What's the matter with you today? Are
you having PMS?" She tiptoed up to hiss the last remark in Bailey's ear.

Bailey turned her haughtiest scowl on her friend, but
thirty years of familiarity had indeed bred contempt.
Jodi laughed.

"I thought you reserved that look for old Mrs. Dun-
nigan. Remember how you used to get her so confused,
she'd have the Mesopotamians pillaging Paris? Come
on, Bailey. Let's go out tonight. We'll even take Samantha. If you don't want to go to the concert, we'll
do something else."

Heaving a deep sigh, Bailey turned to Gordon.
"Would you excuse us a minute?" He waved a hand
negligently, and she shoved Jodi into her bedroom and
closed the door.

"I didn't want to tell you this, but I know who Prince
Charming is," she whispered.

"Is that what's upsetting you? Jeez. I know, too.
I'm not completely retarded."

"It doesn't bother you? I mean, he's a *lawyer*."

"I know, and I swore I'd never get mixed up with
a lawyer, but he's really not a typical lawyer. And he's
gone to so much trouble to convince me of that. I think
it's terribly sweet."

"You like him? I mean, really like him?" Bailey sat

down on the edge of her bed, unable to comprehend what she was hearing.

Jodi smiled in pleased embarrassment. "Yeah," she said. "I really like him."

"Then why the hell don't you tell him and get on with it and quit this nonsense?" *And stop letting me make a fool of myself*, she added silently.

"Are you kidding? I'm having too much fun. Think of it, Bailey, I'm finally in control of a lawyer. He's falling all over himself to please me, and I love it!"

"Jodi! How can you care about him and talk like that?"

"Come on, Bailey. Loosen up a little. He's having as much fun as I am. Why spoil it? I'll tell him when he finally gets around to confessing." Her smile turned wicked. "Or maybe I won't. Maybe I'll act horrified and let him sweat a little."

That, at least, would serve the jerk right, Bailey thought.

"In the meantime, can't you play along, too? I thought you were having fun. I know you like Gordon, and it sort of seemed like you and Austin were getting on better."

Jodi looked so happy, so pleased with herself.

"Sure," Bailey mumbled. "If that's what you want."

Jodi tiptoed up to kiss her friend's cheek. "Thanks. I knew I could count on you. This might be *it*, Bailey. The real thing, I mean."

Oh, brother. This was bad. The only other time Jodi has used the "it" word was about her then future ex-husband, and she'd been sixteen at the time. Since then, the good ones had been "better than the one last week" or "slightly more interesting than Saturday night television."

"I'll change clothes while you call Austin and tell him I'll go to the concert and do the stupid run with him, though I fail to see the purpose of it. The run, that is.''

Jodi laughed. "Austin wants to run with you, and you don't see why? Come on, Bailey. Get real. Competition, of course. The lifeblood of your relationship.''

"Ah. Of course.'' So he thought to make Jodi jealous by running with her friend? Was that why he'd kissed her? What a jerk!

Austin couldn't believe it when Bailey hung up in his ear. He slammed his own receiver down even though it was too late for her to hear. She was, by far, the most confusing woman he'd ever met, as well as the rudest.

What on earth had made him want to run with her anyway? She was no real competition. Even out of shape, he'd beaten her in that first race. So he should just drop it.

Okay, so she'd beaten him at the deposition and the chessboard. He'd won at running, swimming, and cooking. That made it three to two, his favor. Not to mention that he deserved an extra honorary point for eating that awful cheesecake. So that made the score four to two. A good time to quit.

He stalked into the tiny kitchen and gently shook each of the four beers in the refrigerator, selecting the one that seemed the least frozen. Damned apartment. Nothing worked right. Maybe staying in Kansas City wasn't such a hot idea after all. Maybe he'd request a transfer back to St. Louis after things got rolling at the office here. At least at home he had a refrigerator that only made ice in the freezer.

When the phone rang, he took his second sip of beer and considered not answering it. But it might be family or friends back home. Sunday afternoon was prime phone time.

"Austin! This is Jodi. I have a message for you. On behalf of Bailey Russell, I herewith extend her apology and request that the festivities begin.''

That was it? The woman told him to blow it out his ear, then sent her weak apology by proxy?

"I'm sorry, Jodi, but I've already made other plans."

"No, you haven't. Look, Bailey was just upset about something, and she took it out on you. Haven't you ever done that? I'll bet you've done it to your secretary a lot of times."

Austin smiled into the receiver. "You could be right on both counts, but I'm still not going. You and Gordon get along just fine with that impossible woman, so why don't the three of you go together?"

"Because we're the four Musketeers and because Gordon can't possibly handle two women at the same time. Confidentially, I doubt that he could handle even one."

Jodi giggled as Gordon shouted something unintelligible from the background.

"All right," Austin agreed. One more time he'd go along so Gordon could be with Jodi, but only one more. Even friendship had its limits, and tolerating Bailey's bad temper was pushing them.

He hung up the phone and stared at the beer can still clutched in his other hand. Would two sips be enough to impair his running? He poured the remainder down the kitchen sink, then checked his wheat germ to see if it was frozen. Maybe a couple of spoonfuls of the health food would compensate for any ill effects the beer might have on his running.

He was still angry at Bailey, but the prospect of racing with her again blunted the edges of his ire. The adrenaline was already pumping.

The band played Bailey's favorite music, oldies from the sixties and seventies, with a few of the more mellow tunes from the eighties. Under different circumstances, she would have really enjoyed the evening.

Lounging on a blanket spread under a tree, Jodi and

Gordon sipped wine from paper cups, giggling about how awful it was. Bailey was tempted to ask for some . . . a lot, in fact, and forget the blasted run. Somehow the idea of racing Austin no longer appealed to her.

Nor, it would seem, did he have much interest in it. He sat cross-legged, straight-backed, on a front corner of the blanket, apparently absorbed in the music. Anyone observing the group would have doubtless thought Jodi and Gordon were lovers, and she and Austin were recently divorced—from each other.

She supposed Jodi's actions constituted more of this stupid competition she'd mentioned, that Jodi was trying to make Austin jealous. Dumb. Why didn't they just come out with it, be honest and open, instead of playing asinine games?

The band broke into a rendition of "Summer Breeze," a favorite of Bailey's. She relaxed against the rough bark of the tree trunk, feeling the light breeze on her sweat-damp face as the kid playing lead guitar sang about it. There was no jasmine in the air to blow through her mind, but she could smell honeysuckle mixed with the marijuana smoke.

Very softly she began to sing along. Even before she turned and saw Austin watching her, she could feel the heat of his gaze. Embarrassed at being caught singing badly, she refused to let him see her discomfort. One eyebrow raised haughtily, she returned his solemn stare.

"Blink, damn it," Jodi suddenly ordered, waving a hand between the two faces. "Why don't you two go run and tear your knee cartilages or fall on your faces or something? It's a little more socially acceptable than a staring contest."

Austin's expression lightened at that prospect, but Bailey still couldn't engender any enthusiasm. If she'd been by herself, the idea of a run in the approaching twilight would have been soothing, but Austin's presence changed everything. She wanted to go home and lock the door behind her, hide from this awkwardly painful situation with Austin and Jodi.

Instead, as her heart squeezed inside, she laced her shoes tighter, tied them in a double knot, and stood up, stiffly erect. "Ready," she announced.

They walked some distance from the concert.

"Where to?" Austin asked.

Bailey shrugged. "Up to you. I don't think we ought to run around the park and disturb these happy folks, so why don't we circle through the neighborhood in that direction and come back to Gordon's house? It's only a few blocks from here."

The first few steps were almost agony. Bailey's legs seemed heavy and strange, but by the time they left the park, habit or something had taken over. The legs belonged to her again, obeyed her commands, carried her along.

One by one the stars popped out of the dusk, and a full moon turned from pale yellow to bright gold. The moonbeams reached down toward earth, and Bailey exulted in the sensation that she could run right up one directly to the moon.

Austin touched her shoulder and pointed. "Let's grab one and sprint up it," he said, as though reading her mind.

"I'll race you to the moon," she responded.

"You would!" he agreed, and the way he said it made her feel as if one of the beams had lodged its brightness and energy inside her chest. One corner of her mind warned her to reject the feeling, but she allowed it to remain, to mingle with all the other good feelings engendered by running.

She ran easily now, conserving her energy for later, and Austin stayed beside her. She had half expected him to try to keep at least a few paces ahead of her. He wouldn't have challenged her to another race if he hadn't been practicing, hadn't been sure of winning.

However, the real race began when they made the

last turn, and the tall hedge around Gordon's yard loomed in the distance. Bailey wasn't sure if she started increasing her speed first and he followed, or vice versa, or if they started at the same time. At any rate, they ran the last couple of blocks in full sprint.

Bailey was sure her lungs were going to burst and her legs fall off, but she didn't dare slow down. Austin was pulling ahead. He was a good ten paces in front of her when he reached the big tree at the edge of Gordon's property. As his momentum carried him on past, he touched the tree as if in a childhood game, threw his hands into the air, and finally halted on the sidewalk, just inside the opening in the hedge.

Bailey passed the tree in full stride even though she'd lost, then slowed to a stop beside him. "Damn!" she swore, bending over and trying to catch her breath, but it was a halfhearted curse. After a run like that, even the loser was a winner.

"Good race," Austin gasped, flinging an arm companionably about her shoulders.

"Yes," she agreed, her blood racing, heart pounding, and breath coming in labored pants. Her face burned from summer heat without and blood heat within. The breeze tickled her skin without abating the fire.

"You okay?" Austin asked. His hand moved to the back of her neck, his fingers sliding into her damp hair.

She must have overdone it, Bailey thought, because her pulse didn't seem to be slowing.

Raising her head, she looked up at Austin, intending to assure him that she was fine. His bright eyes were dark slits, glittering black in the moonlight. On his upper lip a film of perspiration shimmered. His long fingers drew circles in her hair, on her neck, then his other hand touched her cheek.

Fascinated, unable to look away, Bailey watched his mouth coming toward her, felt herself reach up to meet him. His lips touched hers, generated more heat, released as they both gasped desperately for air, then moved to touch and release and touch again, until the touching seemed more important than breathing.

His lips were soft and firm, giving and demanding. She tasted salt, from him, from herself, opened herself to him as his tongue pushed into her mouth, pulled her into him.

A voice somewhere inside screamed that she shouldn't be kissing Austin, but another voice denied that this was a kiss. It was a continuation of the race, the ultimate high, a total envelopment in sensation.

His damp T-shirt wrinkled maddeningly beneath her exploring hands. She reached impatiently under it to feel the solid width of his back, to touch his skin with her own, to press him closer to her. He returned the pressure, pushed against her, and she moaned into his mouth, exulting in his hardness, in the reactions she had caused in him.

She sucked in a deep, ragged breath, inhaling his musky scent, straining closer, wanting all of him touching her, surrounding her, filling her.

He wedged one hand between them, under her T-shirt, under her athletic bra, and cupped her damp breast, teasing the nipple, sending a bolt of lightning zigzagging through her.

A car whooshed past on the street, and Bailey jumped back, briefly registering that the real world existed only a few feet away. For an instant she wondered just what they were doing, but then Austin's gaze burned into hers. He took her hand, leading her farther inside Gordon's yard, along the thick hedge to the far side of the goldfish pond, behind a large rock formation that completed their retreat from the world of cars and rock concerts.

And the question of what they were doing no longer mattered, she decided, as his hands grasped her hips to bring her back to him. What they were doing didn't matter, only that they continue to do it. Not that she seemed to have much choice; her body would doubtless have run on without her had she tried to stop.

As they sank to the grass, his corded arms wrapped around her, lifted off her shirt and bra. The night air touching her bare skin was cool, but immediately his mouth was there, leaving streaks of fire everywhere he touched—down her neck, around her breasts as he circled and returned to envelop the turgid tip.

She grasped his shoulders, holding on to him, holding him to her. Her heart rate was increasing too fast. Time to slow down, but she couldn't slow down in the middle of the race.

He tugged at the waistband of her shorts, and she leaned back, her hips seeming to rise of their own volition, assisting him to remove the fabric, the barrier that separated his flesh from hers. As he pulled his own shirt off and tossed it aside, she sat up, reached for her shoes, untied the knots, and kicked them off, then turned back to him.

Thick, black hair sprang from the taut muscles of his chest. She moved to him, tangled her fingers in the dark mat. Against her palm she felt his heart pounding surely as fast as her own. Trailing her fingers over his ridged stomach, she stopped at the elastic of his shorts and, holding her breath, daringly slid them downward. He groaned. His hands caught in her hair, kneaded as he whispered her name. She gasped when she guided the fabric down his hard thighs, and saw his readiness, the irrefutable evidence that his fervor ran apace with hers.

She couldn't tell if he lowered her to the grass or she pulled him, but she felt its coolness on her back and the heat of his body over her. His mouth came down on hers again as she opened her thighs to him, moved to meet him, surrounded him as he entered her.

Then they were racing together, and she needed him, wanted him with her all the way. This was no contest, this was the prize, they both won. Together their pace accelerated until they burst into flames and exploded together.

Exhausted, replete, she held on to him, soaking in the feelings, luxuriating in the incredible array of sensations.

Austin held Bailey's slick, sweaty body against his own, kissed her smooth skin, and murmured things he couldn't remember later. Somehow it seemed they would stay forever joined on the soft grass beneath the velvet sky alive with sparkling jewels and flying wisps of clouds. He'd always be able to touch her firm, strong body, lie on her taut stomach, revel in her perfection.

Then sanity slowly returned, and with it the realization that he had just made love outside, under the stars, in Gordon's front yard, only a few blocks from a crowd of people. Being caught like this would make a great entry in his *Martindale-Hubbell* bio.

Still, irrationally, he lingered, savoring the peaceful, satiated look on Bailey's face, the knowledge that he'd brought her to that point. And she'd had an equally devastating effect on him. Giving way to spontaneous lust on his friend's lawn wasn't something he did on a regular basis.

With one finger he touched her smooth skin, traced the line of her high cheekbones. How delicate and helpless she seemed, lying there in the moonlight, her eyes glazed and heavy-lidded as she looked up at him.

A loud drum roll from the nearby concert rumbled through the night, and Bailey's eyes widened, became alert, and he knew they could no longer ignore the world outside. With a final kiss, he rolled away, turned his back to her as he adjusted his clothes, giving them both time to collect themselves.

When his clothes were straight and he'd raked his fingers through his hair, still he didn't face her, didn't know what he ought to say, wasn't even sure what he *wanted* to say. What he wanted to *do* was hold her in his arms again. Taking a deep breath, he turned around to face her.

She was gone.

He kicked the rock structure of the goldfish pond, smashed his toe, cursed roundly.

If that wasn't just like the bloody woman!

He charged off toward the park, finally saw her just as she reached the blanket and sat down, stiffly erect, behind Jodi and Gordon.

"Hi, folks!" Jodi greeted him. "Does this late appearance mean Bailey trounced you in the great race?"

"No," Bailey corrected quietly. "Austin won."

It was only the truth, but he didn't like the way she said it, as if he'd conquered her in some cruel, personal way. He hadn't forced her to make love, and she'd seemed to enjoy it every bit as much as he—and that was a lot.

"Are we ready to go home?" Bailey asked. "The mosquitoes are driving me crazy."

Austin hadn't noticed any mosquitoes, but he had heard they were more attracted to fair-skinned people, and Bailey's skin was very fair, especially in the moonlight.

"Sounds good to me," Gordon agreed. "But the night is young, and so are we."

"No," Bailey said, and the monosyllable was so final, everyone turned their attention to her. "I'm really tired," she explained, but it didn't have the ring of truth. "I have an early appointment in the morning. You all go on if you want to."

She stood up and began folding the blanket. With an exchange of puzzled looks, Austin joined Jodi and Gordon in assisting her.

Damn the woman, Austin thought as they crossed the park. She even made it a point to walk beside Jodi, as far away from him as possible. What was her problem?

He hadn't made love by himself. She'd been a willing participant. More than willing, if memory served him correctly. Surely it wasn't possible the supremely confident Bailey Russell was suffering from embarrassment at her actions.

Whatever the problem, he supposed he had no choice but to back off for the moment.

"We got company," Gordon suddenly announced, and Austin looked up to see two tall figures leaning against Gordon's BMW.

"Excuse me," Gordon said, brushing past the one in front and reaching for the passenger door. Alcohol fumes hung thickly on the night air.

"The nice man said 'excuse me,' " the youth slurred, looking at his friend and laughing. "The nice man with the pretty car." He tipped his glass and poured the remaining liquid over the gleaming hood.

Austin lunged toward the creature, but Gordon held his arm out in front of him, blocking his attack. Austin seethed but backed off.

"This nice car has a wonderful feature, doors on both sides," Gordon said evenly as he took Jodi's arm to steer her around the automobile.

"Isn't that cute? A little girl to go with the little car." The drunk stretched out a hand and touched Jodi's face as she started past him.

Gordon's fist shot out, made a dull *whump* as it connected with the boy's jaw and tumbled him to the ground.

Gordon reached over him and jerked the door open, slamming it against the second drunk's shoulder as he lunged forward, reaching for Gordon.

"And all the doors work just fine." He offered his arm to Jodi.

Daintily Jodi took Gordon's arm, stepped around the youth, and slid into the front car seat.

"You hit him," Austin marveled as both drunks

made a hurried retreat. "You hit him and knocked him down."

"I've been saving my strength," Gordon drawled, closing Jodi's door and moving around to the driver's side. "You two go out and exercise and use it all up, but me, I've been saving it for a lot of years."

With a big, dopey smile, he slid into the car next to Jodi.

Bailey tapped gently on Jodi's bedroom door.

"What is it?" Jodi's reply was muffled but notably irritated as it came through the heavy wood.

"I need to talk to you, Jodi."

The door opened and Jodi stood there frowning, but still cute and darling even in the middle of the night in her short nightgown with her hair tousled. Beside her Bailey felt tall, gaunt, and awkward.

"Bailey, this is the third time you've awakened me to talk about nothing. What *is* the problem? I thought you were tired and wanted to go to bed."

"I am. I do. But I just have to talk to you. Let's go out to the living room."

Jodi followed with a sigh. "So far tonight we've settled the questions of whether or not to have cable TV and where I can buy an air cleaner for Morris' cigar smoke. What is it this time?"

Bailey picked up Samantha and cuddled her. "If you went to the doctor and he discovered you were dying, would you want to know?"

"Sure I'd want to know. Am I dying?" She rubbed her eyes with both hands and yawned, then sat up straight, alert. "You're not sick, are you?"

"No, no," Bailey denied. *At least not physically*, she added silently. Jodi's obvious concern made her feel even worse. She had to tell the truth, no matter what the consequences.

"Okay," she began again, "if you were married and

your husband was cheating on you and I found out, would you want me to tell you?"

"I know for a fact I'm not married, and if you're going to tell me that Steve cheated on me, you're a few years late."

"Jodi, I have to tell you something."

"Bailey, you have exactly ten seconds to tell me before I go to bed with earplugs."

Bailey cleared her throat, shifted Samantha to her shoulder, needing the comfort of the soft little body. Samantha gave her a sleepy lick, then settled comfortably against Bailey's neck. "Jodi, I—Austin and I— we sort of made love." The last words came out in a rush, and she raised her eyes from her lap only long enough to see how Jodi was taking it.

Jodi gaped at her in openmouthed astonishment. "What do you mean, you sort of made love? Did you or didn't you?"

"We did," Bailey admitted miserably. "In Gordon's yard."

"You don't mean for real. You're being metaphorical, right?"

"I'm sorry. We just got carried away by the race, I guess. It all sort of flowed from one thing to the other. I'm so sorry." She forced herself to meet Jodi's eyes. To her relief, there were no tears.

"Wait a minute. You mean you and Austin got it on in Gordon's yard, tonight, while the band played on?" Jodi actually seemed to be enjoying this.

"Something like that."

"I don't believe it."

"I'm afraid it's true."

"Why are you so upset? Was it terrible? Come on, tell me all the details!" Jodi leaned closer, grinning impishly.

"I will not!" Bailey exclaimed. "How can you possibly want to know about your lover making love with another woman? That's sick, Jodi, very sick."

"My lover? Wait a minute. You're not saying you think Austin is Prince Charming?" She collapsed back onto the sofa in gales of laughter.

"I saw him put those flowers in your car! And when I told you, you said you already knew he was Prince Charming!" Bailey defended herself.

"I did no such thing! Maybe he put the flowers in my car, but Gordon bought them, believe me. I saw the receipt in his car. Prince Charming is Gordon, the wonderful man who fought for me tonight. Have you ever had a man fight for you? It's really an incredible feeling. Probably every bit as great as that runner's high you keep babbling about."

Bailey's head was spinning, trying to assimilate all the ramifications of this new information. "You're not in love with Austin? He's not in love with you?" *He's not using me to get close to you?*

"Of course not. Austin? Are you kidding?"

"Why not Austin? What's wrong with him?" The words came out of her mouth before she could stop them. With a start, she realized she was defending the wretched man.

"I don't know. You tell me. You're the one who's all upset after making love with him. You and Austin, splendor in the grass." She rolled her eyes and laughed. "I love it!"

"Jodi, I have to go to bed now. I'm really tired."

"You got it, kid," Jodi agreed, grinning broadly. "Wait till I tell Gordon," she said as she headed for her bedroom door.

"I'll kill you," Bailey promised.

Jodi laughed, shook her head, and muttered, "Incredible," before closing her door behind her.

Bailey sat on the sofa stroking Samantha. She had to think about this new development. Austin had apparently made love to her because he wanted to. She had participated wholeheartedly, then refused to speak to him. He'd probably hate her for the rest of his life, and that was likely all for the best since they couldn't get along anyway.

But it didn't feel like it was for the best.

"Oh, Samantha," she murmured, holding the little face against her cheek. "I think we've got problems."

SEVEN

"Power suits!" Bailey exclaimed as she threw the third one onto her bed.

She'd never noticed until she started dressing that Monday morning how austere most of her wardrobe was. Other than the suits, several pairs of blue jeans, and a rack of T-shirts from competitive runs, all she had was the dress her mother had given her for her last birthday, the one she'd worn to Gordon's on Saturday night.

Samantha vaulted onto the bed and sniffed the pile.

"However, severe colors and somber lines are necessary for the old career, and that's what's important. Right?"

Samantha pawed daintily at a navy blue pinstripe lapel, tilted her nose into the air, then curled into a ball on the jacket.

"Nobody likes a know-it-all," Bailey quipped, pulling out an old faithful black suit. If she left the top button on her blouse open, maybe it would lessen the severity.

She donned the outfit and studied her image in the dresser mirror. Eyes and hair sitting atop a black tube. Lips and face so pale as to be almost invisible.

Except—she peered closer—for a couple of freckles on her nose. Damn! The sun made her hair redder, but did it give her face any color? Not unless you counted the freckles.

A few minutes in the bathroom with her limited supply of cosmetics helped a little. The foundation was so old, she had to add water to be able to use it. The freckles still seemed to stand out, and the blusher made her look like a clown. She washed her face.

"Jodi!" She charged through the door to find her friend sitting at the dining room table, holding a cup of coffee in one hand, her head cradled in the other.

Jodi peered at Bailey through half-closed eyes, then broke into a sleepy but smug grin. "Good morning. Did you have pleasant dreams last night?"

"Open your eyes. Look at me."

Jodi shrugged. "I can see you."

"So what can I do? I look terrible."

Jodi sat up straight, took a drink of coffee, and studied Bailey for a moment, then shrugged again. "You look like you always look, except your blouse is unbuttoned."

Bailey threw her arms into the air. "So I always look awful, is that what you're saying?"

"Oh, now I get it," Jodi drawled, staggering to her feet. "Come with me. I've got just the thing for you."

Thirty minutes later, hair fluffy from electric curlers, a brightly patterned scarf lending color to her suit, and soft shadows and mascara making her eyes seem larger than ever, Bailey studied herself in the hall bathroom mirror.

The makeup was okay. She still looked like herself, but like the new, improved version. Trouble was, she felt like the same old Bailey inside. If she looked prettier, shouldn't she feel prettier?

Jodi appeared in the mirror behind her, straightened the scarf, and draped an arm around her shoulders. "Now you just need to act more like a lady, and Austin will be bowled over by your new look and new outlook.''

''What makes you think this has anything to do with Austin?'' Was she so obvious?

''Oh, just coincidentally the morning after you make love with a man, you suddenly start worrying about your appearance.''

Bailey's leg muscles seemed to wilt, and she sank onto the edge of the bathtub. She was being blatantly silly. This wouldn't do at all. She had to regain control, approach and deal with this strange attraction in a rational, intelligent manner.

She stood, leaned over the sink, turned on the water, and grabbed a bar of soap.

''What are you doing?'' Jodi snatched the soap away from her.

''Getting ready to wash my face so I can go to work.''

''Bailey, what's the matter with you? What's so horrible about being in love? I always enjoy it myself, even if it only lasts for a few minutes—until I get to know the guy with the great smile who turns out to have the personality of a cardboard cutout.''

''Don't be absurd. How could I possibly love a man who argues with everything I say?'' Bailey started to brush past her friend, to go to her own bathroom and wash her face, but Jodi grabbed her arm.

''Right. Making love with men you don't care about is something you do on a regular basis. Bailey Russell, you seem to forget you're talking to someone who remembers you from pre-training-pants days. So cut the garbage.''

Bailey sighed, then shrugged, deciding to admit to half the truth. ''I saw myself in the mirror this morning, and I didn't like it,'' she finally said. ''Maybe I'm having a midlife crisis a little early, that's all. As for being in love, you, of all people, should know that's something I don't do very well.''

"You haven't practiced much, that's for sure." Jodi plopped onto the side of the tub, patting the area beside her. "Sit here and talk to me."

Reluctantly Bailey joined her. "What's to talk about? I think I've always been a realistic person, capitalized on my strong points, worked around the weaknesses. While I'm a fairly good attorney and a decent runner, I'd have made a lousy opera singer. We all lack abilities in certain areas. Relationships with parties of the opposite sex is one of my areas."

"And just why do you suppose that is?"

At least Jodi hadn't come across with any reassuring clichés.

"How do I know why? Why don't I have a voice suitable for the opera? Why can't I run a four-minute mile?"

"Think, Bailey. Use that brain you're so proud of. Consider that you're a beautiful, successful, bright woman."

"Okay, now you're getting into the con job. If I'm beautiful, how come men never ask me out? No, Jodi, I'm not pretty like you, and I don't know what to say to interest a man. I gave up trying a long time ago, and I will not make a fool—a bigger fool—of myself with Austin. Now, I'm going to wash my face and go to work, and the subject is closed."

She stood up, but Jodi's voice stopped her from leaving.

"No, you're not pretty like me. I'm cute; you're drop-dead gorgeous in spite of the way you dress and chop your hair. The reason men don't ask you out is because you're obnoxious."

Bailey whirled in amazement. "I am not!"

Jodi shrugged. "Okay. Will you settle for competitive and intimidating? What man could possibly feel like he's a match for you except maybe Austin?"

"Austin and I are natural enemies. We can't be together five minutes without fighting."

"Not quite true," Jodi disagreed. "What you two do is compete, something that's as natural as breathing for both of you. But lighten up a little. Try to hold it down to ninety percent of the time. Play nice once in a while."

Bailey stood in the doorway, trying to take in what Jodi had said, to decide if any of it had validity, if it mattered.

"Go on and wash your face," Jodi finally added, waving her hand dismissively. "The makeup isn't integral to the situation, anyway. Only if it makes you feel different about yourself."

Austin leaned across the conference table, his heart pounding as furiously as if he had been in a race.

"Right here in Article Three," he said, pointing with his gold ball-point pen.

Stafford Morris nodded slowly. The man actually seemed to be considering the merger offer. At least he hadn't rejected it, and he hadn't blown smoke in Austin's face even once.

Morris flipped through the papers, then folded them and stood. "I'll read through your offer," he promised, "and submit it to the other partners for consideration."

Austin nodded agreeably. "Certainly. I think you'll find it advantageous for both firms. You have some good attorneys, some old-line clients, but you're not taking new ground like we are. The legal field is changing. It's a business, has to be run like a business. We plan to be so large that we'll handle all our clients' needs, have a department for everything. One-stop shopping."

Stafford listened quietly, then took a cigar out of his shirt pocket and lit up. Squinting through the smoke, he grinned around the rolled tobacco, leisurely took it from his mouth. "I'll look it over. Daniel . . ." He nodded to the older man across the table. "Good to see you. Give my best to Rose."

At the elevator, Daniel Lewis was distracted by another client, and Austin seized the opportunity. "This merger would be very interesting for me," he told Morris. "I applied for a position with your firm when I got out of law school. Gordon and I came in together."

"I remember," Morris said evenly. "You were all wound up and ready to conquer the world. A lot like the young lady I'd just hired, Bailey Russell. I knew one of you was enough, and I was right. It takes Gordon to balance with her."

Austin wasn't sure he was hearing right. "You're saying you hire lawyers on the basis of personality?"

Morris blew smoke just to the right of Austin's ear. The man was smiling, not with his mouth, but with all the rest of his face. "A law firm's like a family. Everybody has a different role, but they all have to work together. It's not a machine you can plug available parts into." The elevator doors opened, and Morris stepped on, turned, and lifted one hand in a wave to Lewis, but his words were for Austin. "You were too damned pushy then. You're still too damned pushy."

The doors closed. After several seconds, Austin blinked, turned, and headed back to his office.

He had lost out on the job because he would have clashed with Bailey, because Morris considered him as pushy as she was, not because he wasn't bright enough or didn't have enough honors or good enough grades. He had been rejected because he tried too hard. He needed to think about that for a while.

Slumping into his chair, he pulled up to his desk and stared sightlessly at the papers in front of him. It was not, he believed, possible to be "too damned pushy" in the legal field. Morris was wrong about that. Anyway, the man was as pushy as they came. He apparently just had a problem with perception.

Austin leaned back in his chair, lifted his feet to his desk. So he hadn't really lost on getting that job. Morris had made a judgmental decision based on his skewed perception of the problem.

Maybe not so skewed after all. He and Bailey couldn't seem to get along. But that had to be her fault, not his. The other women he'd dated hadn't acted like her. They didn't argue with him every time he opened his mouth. They didn't try to win at every game or sport. They didn't have some smart answer for everything. They didn't make him feel vital and alive. They didn't have big green eyes, soft, full lips, fiery hair, a sleek body—

Austin caught himself smiling. Okay, so Bailey wasn't a typical female, and he got pretty irritated with her sometimes. Nevertheless, there was definitely an attraction. And, damn it, he knew she felt it, too, in spite of her inexplicable actions after the most incredible lovemaking he'd ever experienced, actions that had kept him awake half the night trying to figure out what had gone wrong.

He flipped forward in his chair. If he was pushy, then so be it. He'd call Bailey and ask her outright what the problem was. He snatched up the phone and dialed the number for Hoskins, Grier. But when the receptionist answered, he swallowed twice, then asked to speak to Gordon.

Well, that should prove Stafford Morris was wrong. He couldn't even push himself into a confrontation with Bailey.

"Busy for lunch?" he asked when Gordon answered. The three of them at lunch, that would be a safe situation. He could work up from there.

"I'm trying to get a brief put together, so I guess I'll just have my secretary bring me a sandwich today."

Austin hesitated, then laughed. "Very funny. How about we go over to the hotel and have a leisurely lunch? I guess your prickly friend will be there, too. Bailey, I mean. And that's fine. I don't have any problem with that."

"Austin, I'm not making a joke. This thing's been on my desk forever, and I need to finish it. It's time for me to get serious about my career, make something of myself. I'm thirty years old, and what have I done with my life?"

Since it was unlikely somebody was holding a gun to Gordon's head to make him say those things, there must be a logical reason. "If you're worried about the merger, don't be."

"I'm not worried about the merger. Look, you've always worked this hard. It's about time I got started. Anyway, when Jodi finds out her Prince Charming is not only an attorney, but an unsuccessful attorney, she may not be very charmed."

The man was serious. Since Austin had been preaching to Gordon for years about buckling down, he couldn't understand the bleak feeling that settled over him, as if he'd just lost a friend.

"Good for you," he said, though his words sounded phony even to himself. "So how about a few drinks after work?"

"I'll probably be staying here late. Maybe another time."

Austin hung up the phone, feeling suddenly alone.

He drummed his fingers on his desk, shuffled a few papers, then decided to wander over to the deli at lunch and see if Bailey was there. Maybe check out a couple of the local places, too. An accidental meeting would work.

Bailey couldn't believe what she was hearing. She'd finally found Gordon in the library, taking notes from a lawbook. That was strange enough, but then he'd actually told her, with a straight face, that he was going to work through lunch.

Of all days for him to have a psychosis! She'd worn the bloody makeup to work and even received a few scattered compliments, but if Gordon wouldn't help her get within Austin's viewing range, how would she ever know if he approved? And how could she possibly be nice to the man if she couldn't get within speaking distance of him?

"I'll help you with that work later," she offered. "Let's go eat. I'm starving. And you need a break. You can't work continually. Wears your brain out."

"You're one to talk! How many times have I tried to pry you out of your office? Now it's my turn. Go away and let me concentrate."

He returned his attention to the legal tome in front of him, and Bailey moved away from the door.

"You look nice today," he called after her.

Great, she thought. I look nice today. But it's a cinch this blasted makeup won't last through the night.

Maybe she should treat this like any other incident in her life and take the bull by the horns. Call Austin and see if he wanted to . . . what? After last night, even asking him to go for a run might sound suggestive. A noon date, with its connotations, was clearly out of the question.

She marched back into her office, slumped in her chair, and ground her teeth. Okay, so she couldn't count on Gordon to help. How else could she arrange for an accidental meeting? Maybe she could kind of wander through the area restaurants at lunch, and if she saw him eating, he might ask her to join him. If he didn't—and he might not after the rude way she'd acted the night before—well, she'd cross that bridge when she came to it. No need inventing problems before they arose.

Bailey looked from the prepared sandwiches, squashed in their cellophane wrappers, to her reflection in the mirror behind the counter. The sandwiches pretty much reflected the way she looked and felt, except they were cool in their refrigerated case, and she couldn't recall ever having been hotter.

She'd never before realized there were so many places to eat within walking distance of the office, and not a sign of Austin in any of them. Just as well, she thought, staring back at the creature in the mirror, the one with a shiny, flushed face, flattened hair, and raccoon eyes.

"Chicken salad sandwich," she told the clerk as he approached her. Accepting the shapeless lump, she gave the man a five-dollar bill.

"Well, hello."

Bailey jumped at the sound of the voice behind her and whirled to see Austin. He looked cool and crisp in his white, short sleeved shirt, tie loose at his throat, jacket draped over his shoulder. She felt frumpy and disheveled.

"Hi, yourself. Out for a little lunch?" Great conversation, stupid, she berated herself. What else would he be doing in a deli at this time of day?

"Yes," he answered politely. "Care to join me?"

They both looked down at the sandwich she was clutching so hard, her fingers were making indentations.

"Your change, ma'am," the man behind the counter announced, extending a pudgy hand beside her face.

"Oh!" Distractedly she folded the dollar bills and the sandwich and dropped everything into her shoulder bag. Only when she saw the puzzled look on Austin's face as his gaze followed her actions did she realize what she'd done.

This wasn't going at all well. She had to get out of there. "Well, got to run," she stammered. "Nice to see you again."

Proud of herself for at least remembering her manners, she stretched her dry lips into a smile. In an attempt to maintain some semblance of poise, she wheeled away from him in a Ginger Rogers–type twirl, but somehow both feet ended up in the same spot. She staggered forward, caught her balance on a table, and race-walked toward the door, afraid to look back.

"Bailey!"

Austin's voice was the last thing she heard as she plunged onto the sidewalk. The steamy heat slapped her in the face about the same time she realized her polite gesture was meaningless since she hadn't even replied to Austin's invitation. In addition to being a total klutz, she'd been unconscionably rude—again. She definitely had no business trying to play this boy-girl game. She'd best get on with the things she knew how to do or, at least, was capable of learning.

But even as she beat a retreat to her office, her sanctuary, an irritating thought niggled at her, a thought that she wasn't going to give up. Whether running, swimming, or making love, the way Austin set all her senses spinning, made her feel she'd just conquered Mount Everest, was enough to keep her trying to win.

The incessant ringing of the telephone finally broke into Bailey's concentration, and she realized it was the night number. She switched the "ring" selector on her phone to "off." She had better things to do than play receptionist.

"Why doesn't somebody answer the damn phone?"

Bailey started at the unexpected voice. Gordon drooped in her doorway.

"What are you doing here?" she asked. "Did you fall asleep in the library "

"I've been working. Are you aware that the phone has been ringing forever?" He leaned against the doorframe, a familiar pose, except now he looked exhausted instead of casual.

"The receptionist goes home at six," Bailey informed him. "If the noise bothers you, either turn your phone off or answer the blasted thing. Those are your choices. Hanging around and complaining is not on the list."

"I tried to answer it, but all I got was a dial tone."

"Punch in seven-two. It came out in a memo when

we got the new system three years ago. I think it's quit ringing, though, so your question is moot.'' Bailey closed the file in front of her, and her voice softened. ''You look terrible. I don't believe I've ever seen you tired before.''

Gordon shoved his hands into his pockets and smiled. ''I think I've found out what makes you so grumpy. Work. Come on, I'll walk you to the parking lot. That way, if anyone attacks us, you can save us. I'm too weak.''

Bailey took Gordon's arm. ''Let's go, old buddy. I'll keep you safe from the monsters.''

As they left the building, it occurred to Bailey that if she and Gordon were there, Jodi was home alone. ''How about we stop by my place and have a couple? I'm sure Samantha and Jodi would love to see you.''

Gordon brightened momentarily, then shook his head. ''I'm dead. All I want to do is make it inside my front door and pass out on the carpet.''

Bailey paused beside her car. ''What brought all this on, Gordon? Did Stafford come down on you? His ire has never bothered you before.''

Gordon shrugged. ''It's time I made something of myself.''

Bailey stretched up to kiss his scratchy cheek and surprised herself by saying, ''There's nothing wrong with the old Gordon. I kind of like him. Don't force yourself to be something you're not.''

Gordon shook his head. ''I wish you people would make up your minds,'' he grumbled. As he walked away, he called over his shoulder, ''Tell your room-mate . . . tell her I'll see her tomorrow.''

Well, Bailey thought as she turned her ignition key, I'm not the only one having an early midlife crisis.

She arrived home to find Jodi and Samantha watching television. Jodi was polishing her toenails and had just finished Samantha's, as Bailey discovered when the dog leaped into her arms and lay back, feet in the air, showing off her pedicure. Obviously this midlife crisis was contagious, an airborne microorganism likely.

Jodi immediately muted the sound on the television. "You got a phone call," she sang out.

"Good. That means they haven't turned off my service." Bailey grabbed a beer from the refrigerator, kicked off her shoes, and joined Jodi on the sofa.

"Austin phoned to see if you wanted to go for a drink. I told him he could probably catch you at the office. Did he get you before you left? You ought to call him back if he didn't."

Bailey hated herself for the surge of delight she felt at Jodi's news. "Did he say I should call back?" she asked, keeping her attention focused on rubbing Samantha's tummy.

"Not exactly," Jodi admitted, "but it's a perfect excuse."

"If I wanted to phone Austin, which I don't, but if I did, I would simply do so. I don't need an excuse to call someone."

"Suit yourself." Jodi turned the sound back up on the sitcom unfolding on the television screen.

Bailey reached for the remote control and muted the noise again. "What, exactly, did he say?"

Jodi turned to face Bailey, her eyes dancing. "First he asked for Gordon, but I could tell it was just a ruse."

"How could you tell it was just a ruse?" Bailey interrupted, her happiness fading at the knowledge he had really been calling to find Gordon.

"He sounded unsure of himself. That's not like Austin."

"No," Bailey agreed, "it's not like Austin to be unsure of himself. But it is like Jodi to read in things that aren't really there."

"Not so. Anyway, to continue, hopefully without interruption, I told him Gordon wasn't here, then he said if you and I weren't doing anything, maybe we'd like to go for a drink. I told him you weren't here, but he should try the office, and I gave him the night number.''

Bailey thought of the ringing phone she hadn't answered. The delight came surging back.

"I'll treat for dinner if you'll do my makeup tomorrow," Bailey offered. Just in case he called again.

Jodi leaned back on the sofa, laughed, and wiggled her red toenails in the air. "We never grow up, do we? We just get older." She turned to Bailey. "Let me paint your toenails, too. Men love painted toenails."

Bailey jerked her feet up under her and held Samantha protectively. "You're crazy. Go put your shoes on or I won't be seen in public with you."

But when Jodi left the room, she stretched out one foot and tried to imagine it with crimson toenails, tried to decide if men—one man in particular—might find them appealing. Nuts, she chided herself. You're losing your mind and all sense of decorum and going totally nuts.

When Bailey arrived in her office the next morning, the first thing she did was turn the ring switch of her phone back on. A few minutes later when it shrilled at her, she jumped involuntarily, then snatched it up.

"Bailey Russell."

"You sound awful damn happy for this hour of the morning," Stafford Morris growled. "Come see me."

The connection was broken.

Probably another lease for Larry Haynes. Doing that man's work ought to be worth a partnership if she did nothing else.

She stopped by the kitchen for a caffeine refill, then moved on to the big corner office. Jodi looked up from a document she was proofing when Bailey came by.

"I've been summoned to the lion's den," she said in answer to Jodi's questioning look. "If I don't come back, take care of Samantha, but leave her toenails alone.''

She knocked on the door, then opened it and entered. Just as she was closing it, he growled, "Close the door."

This could be serious.

When she left fifteen minutes later, she had to do a visual check to be sure her feet were touching the floor. Winking at Jodi, she floated on down the hallway.

She was being offered a partnership at the end of the month. The official announcement would be made at the fiscal-year-end party, but she was unofficially invited to attend a special partners' meeting before work the next morning. Stafford Morris had actually said he valued her input and wanted her to be involved in the meeting. Words of gold!

When the phone rang again a few minutes later, and she heard Austin's voice, her already intense excitement spiraled.

"I thought maybe we ought to get together and go over certain aspects of the Candy Miller case," he said, his tone distant.

"Sure," Bailey agreed, feeling a little confused, her excitement whorling away. Was that why he had tried to call her the night before? "My office or yours?"

"Actually, I thought we might meet somewhere neutral. How about Reilly's?"

"Good," she agreed, smiling to the ceiling. Meeting in a bar didn't sound very business-oriented. She allowed her mind to linger on Sunday night, on the wild, ecstatic feelings his touch, his lovemaking, had evoked in her, and for the first time, she dared to anticipate those feelings again.

EIGHT

Locating Austin was easy, even in the after-work crowd at Reilly's. Admiring his dark hair, good looks, and aura of self-assurance, Bailey was surprised everyone in the place wasn't looking at him. At that thought, twin thrills zigged along her spine—one of exultation that this "hunk" was waiting for her, and one of fear that he couldn't possibly be interested in her.

As she walked toward his table, a waitress paused beside him, and he looked up at the woman, smiling as he spoke. Bailey experienced a pang of something she reluctantly had to admit was jealousy. Hesitating a moment, she took a deep breath and plunged on. No use kidding herself. Her normal confidence took a vacation when it came to male/female relationships, especially when Austin was the male.

But the smile he turned on her when he saw her approaching went a long way toward restoring it. Now, *that* was a smile, not the imitation he'd given the waitress.

"Hi," he said, standing up and pulling out a chair for her. "I ordered you a glass of white wine. I was afraid we might not see another waitress for a while.

We can send it back if you'd rather have something else.''

She could use something a little stronger—say, a dozen tequila shooters. ''Thank you,'' she said. ''White wine will be fine.'' Great, she thought. You've sunk to lousy poetry. A surefire way to impress the man.

The waitress returned, set a beer in front of Austin and a glass of pale liquid in front of Bailey. She immediately took a shaky gulp, then set the glass down so abruptly, the wine sloshed onto her hand. Smooth move, klutz, she berated herself. Maybe if she sort of waved her hand around unobtrusively while she talked, it would dry and Austin wouldn't notice.

''Well,'' she said, flinging her hand out, ''what's new with our little insurance case?''

Austin's expression was confused for a moment, and an absurd happiness sang through her veins. Jodi had been right. He hadn't called her to talk about the case. She battled with her lips to keep them from bursting into a sappy grin.

''Nothing significant,'' he finally answered.

What should she say to that? It was her turn, and her mind was a blank. Nervousness had stolen her happiness. ''Done any more running lately?'' Way to go! Now he'll think you're being suggestive. ''Alone, I mean.'' No, that was worse! ''In the daylight.'' *Oh, jeez!* ''Hot weather for running.'' She grabbed her wine and shoved the glass into her mouth. Anything to stop it from talking. She was making a total fool of herself. The man would never want to see her again.

''No, I haven't done any more running, not since we—not in the last couple of days,'' he answered. ''Been really busy at the office. How about you?''

''Yes. Me, too. Really busy.'' Such eloquence. She badly needed a new mouth, or a new brain to control the old one.

''Why don't we have some dinner?'' Austin suggested. ''You haven't eaten yet, have you?''

Sure, they always serve dinner at law offices, Bailey started to say, but remembered Jodi's advice and managed to stop the words before they escaped. "No," she replied, smiling and reaching for her wine.

A large gentleman staggered backward from the burgeoning crowd, into their table, splashing more wine on her hand. As she and Austin grabbed the table to steady it, the man grunted and disappeared back into his group.

The incident caused them to shift just enough so Bailey's knee was pressing against Austin's. Her heart began to hammer. Even through the layers of clothes, she could feel excruciatingly wonderful tingles.

Nevertheless, she started to move away from the accidental touch, then stopped. Maybe it wasn't an accident on his part. He'd think she was rejecting him if she pulled away. But if it was an accident and she didn't move, then what would he think of her? On the other hand, *he* certainly wasn't moving.

With a forced laugh, she waved her dripping hand in the air. "Some people are such knees—needless—heedless!"

Oh, jeez! She hadn't really said that. Please, God, she hadn't really said that.

"No harm done," Austin replied.

Just how did he mean that? Harm done to, and by, whom? Her leg froze. She couldn't have budged it if someone had yelled, "Fire."

Austin half turned in his chair to signal the waitress, but his knee didn't move.

Bailey had never before realized there were so many nerve endings in her knee, and that they led upward into so many other, seemingly unconnected, parts of her body. She was suddenly very aware of the tips of her breasts pushing against the soft fabric of her bra. Her breathing came rapid and shallow, a far cry from her normal slow, deep, athletic respiration.

When the menus arrived, she opened hers and pretended to study it intently, though the print refused to focus.

"What are you having?" Austin asked, closing his menu.

She always got the same thing, but at the moment, she couldn't remember what it was. "Oh, anything. Whatever you're having. I'm easy." She flinched inwardly as she heard the last words escape from her treacherous mouth.

But Austin didn't seem to notice. He appeared relaxed and in control as he lifted his glass of beer to his lips. Was it possible he hadn't noticed the contact? His leg seemed to move slightly, press closer to hers. Or maybe it was only her imagination conjuring up what she wanted.

"Excuse me, I have to find the ladies' room," she blurted out, leaping up from the table.

"More wine?" he asked, indicating her almost empty glass.

"No. Iced tea." If she couldn't control herself on one glass of wine, she'd better not have any more.

In the ladies' room she closeted herself in a cubicle and leaned against the wall. Maybe she could just stay there forever. This was worse than high school, more humiliating. Because, she realized, it was more important. Being popular in school mattered, but not as much as impressing someone special, making that person like you. And, heaven help her, she wanted Austin to like her. She wanted him to look at her again the way he had that night in the park.

She drew in a deep breath and thrust her chin forward. She'd never reach the finish line with an attitude like that. She would go back out there and be so sweet and so clever, he'd forget the first part of the evening. She could do it. Hadn't her motto always been: If someone else could do it, so could she, and just a little bit better?

Shoulders back, she pushed open the door, stepped

out, saw herself in the mirror above the sink, and groaned. Makeup certainly had a short half-life.

Waiting for Bailey to return, Austin leaned back in his chair, his heart racing. Damn the woman! She had him incredibly aroused just by touching his leg. It was a good thing there weren't any bushes around to throw her behind or he'd probably lose control again.

Though he wasn't sure she would be so receptive this time. She seemed bored with the whole evening, didn't even want another drink.

He still didn't understand her recent actions—running away from him, physically and emotionally, after making love on Sunday night; appearing totally confused but no longer angry at lunch on Monday; and now, seemingly eager to meet him here, allowing his leg to touch hers, then bolting from the room. She was a very frustrating woman, weaving—no, make that *crashing*—her way into the core of his being, then retreating frostily.

Lifting his glass, he drained the last few sips of his beer, his mind registering peripherally that it had gone flat and stale. He usually left that last half inch, but Bailey had driven him to unusual behavior.

Across the room he saw her coming back to the table, elegant litheness moving through the chaos.

His fist clenched tightly. He would take charge of the situation, force sense from this chaos. With a macho gesture, he raised his beer glass to his lips and tossed his head back. As Bailey reached the table, he set it back down, hoping in the dim light she hadn't noticed he'd tried to drink from an empty glass.

After an hour of excruciatingly painful mundane conversation, Austin had to admit he was floundering. Bailey totally unnerved him, sitting there all prim and proper in her navy blue pinstripe suit, when he knew what was under it. He'd seen her cool eyes become slits of passion, had kissed her full lips and held her firm, sweaty body against his. However hard she tried to pretend it hadn't happened, he knew it had.

Austin shifted uncomfortably in his chair. "Would you like to go somewhere else?" he asked. "Maybe we could find someplace to dance." He could hold her body next to his again, and who knew what might happen then?

"Dance?" She looked confused, almost frightened. Her eyes darted across the room, then back to him and down to her empty tea glass. "I don't dance," she finally said, her tone cold.

Right, he thought. She could run like a gazelle, swim like a mermaid, make love like—there was no metaphor for that, for the way her body moved so smoothly with his. No woman that coordinated, that graceful, would be unable to dance.

"Religious preference?" he asked sarcastically.

"No. Lack of training." Her eyes met his, defiant, challenging. She sat upright in her chair and crossed her arms.

He knew that body language. She was shutting him out, and as usual, he had no idea why, but he wasn't about to let her know that. He emulated her posture. "How amazing that a beautiful woman like you can't dance."

He almost got her that time. She blinked twice, rapidly, then regained her composure. Austin waited, a strange intoxication pervading his being. He could almost predict what she would say now, and that was exciting, to think he knew her so well. She'd make some snide remark such as how they ought to report that amazing fact to *Ripley's Believe It or Not*.

"Not all of us are skilled in all things," she said.

Austin dropped his gaze to the dirty dishes on the table and took a deep breath, trying to regroup. He'd been wrong. He didn't know her after all.

"I'm sure you have a busy schedule tomorrow," she

continued in that same distant tone, ''and I need to get home and feed Samantha.''

She opened her bag and pulled out her wallet. With another jolt, Austin realized she intended to pay for her own meal.

''No!'' He grabbed her hand, and for an exhilarating instant he could see green sparks shooting from her eyes. ''My treat,'' he insisted. ''You can have me over for dinner next time.''

Blast! Of all things to say to a woman who couldn't cook!

She shrugged and withdrew her hand from his grasp. ''Then thank you for dinner.'' Her eyes dripped green icicles.

''He hates me,'' Bailey informed Jodi an hour later as the two of them perched cross-legged on Jodi's bed, sipping hot chocolate. The scene, reminiscent of so many in high school, was vaguely comforting in spite of the chunk of granite that had settled in her abdominal region after the disastrous evening with Austin. ''Even though I was so nice to him, it would have turned your stomach—it did mine. He hates me.''

''You haven't told me one thing that would substantiate that theory,'' Jodi replied.

''You weren't there to hear the intonations, see the gestures. Anyway, it doesn't matter. I don't care.'' Even with Jodi she should salvage some of her damaged pride.

Jodi raised an eyebrow in disbelief, and Bailey averted her gaze. ''So why did he ask you out if he doesn't like you?'' she asked, ignoring Bailey's last comment.

''I don't know.'' Bailey leaned over the edge of the bed to catch Samantha in midleap. The little dog wriggled from her grasp and nestled into the pillows, midway between the two women. Bailey tangled her fingers in the soft fur, soaking up the undemanding love. ''I don't pretend to understand the man's motives," she said. "Maybe he's up to something underhanded."

Jodi sighed exaggeratedly. "If you'd only apply the same principles to having a relationship that you apply to everything else, you'd have Austin or any other man you choose eating out of your hand. Pull out all the stops, don't quit until the race is over, give it the Bailey Russell effort."

"The race is over, and I could care less. The subject of Austin is closed." She would put him out of her head as well as out of the conversation. She'd had enough of making a fool of herself over a man. Okay, so this particular man made her feel all tingly inside when he touched her, and being with him, competing with him, even when she lost, made her feel as if she were bursting with sunshine and fire. So what? She'd been doing just fine before she met him, and she'd do just fine without him. His only position in her life would be opposing counsel. "It's your turn," she told Jodi. "Tell me what's going on with Prince Charming."

"Ah, Prince Charming." Jodi leaned back against the headboard. "Prince Charming has been far too busy with duties of his kingdom to pay attention to an ordinary commoner."

Bailey sipped her chocolate, but it had gone cold. "Are you saying he's working too much and ignoring you?"

"Except that we know Gordon never works too much. Gordon does the minimum and smiles a lot."

Bailey set her cup on Jodi's nightstand and leaned back against the pillow. "Not true," she said, delighted to be able to disagree after having her earlier comments debunked. "I have personally observed the man at work, as well as the ill effects of this hard work. I told you how tired he was last night."

"Bailey, dear friend, you never have lived in the

same world as the rest of us. Did you know I had an affair with Ron Sims?''

Bailey sat bolt-upright in bed and studied Jodi's face for signs of teasing. "Your old boss? A lawyer? No way. You did not.'' She hesitated. "Did you?''

Jodi's head tilted back, her eyes toward the ceiling. "It happened right after Steve and I got divorced. Haywood isn't exactly brimming with eligible men over the age of eighteen. I guess mostly it was an ego trip, since I'd always been an outsider looking in on Ron's social life.'' She raised a restraining hand. "Before you go making something melodramatic out of it, let me say emphatically that at no time did I ever fancy I loved the jerk. When he told me he was engaged to the mayor's daughter, I heaved a sigh of relief. But the creep thought we'd just keep carrying on together. I didn't like his attitude. So I left.''

"I see,'' Bailey mused, finally understanding Jodi's sudden decision to move to the city.

"I don't like attorneys,'' Jodi continued. "Never have. And I was right, you see. Okay, I admit I lost my head temporarily. Gordon didn't seem like a real lawyer at first, but he is. Maybe he hasn't found someone else on his social level to marry, but he's using his work as an excuse to divert him.''

"You think Gordon's working this hard to avoid you?'' Bailey asked in amazement. "You're nuts. No wonder my life is suddenly so weird. I've been taking advice from a fruitcake. Just because you had a bad experience with a slimeball, you make these sweeping assumptions. This isn't like you.''

"Why? Because I've learned when to throw in the towel?''

"Just a minute ago you were on my case not to quit before the end of the race and a bunch of other drivel in that vein. Put those red toenails in your mouth, did you?'' she gloated.

"I'm not as competitive as you are. I never have been."

"You didn't have to be. You just had to be you. Every guy in high school was after you."

"Well, this isn't high school. I'm thirty years old, not sixteen, and I'm not the head cheerleader anymore. I made a slight judgment error, and now it's time to retreat and go to Plan B."

"That's the Jodi I know," Bailey approved. "What's Plan B?"

"Some more responses to my ad came today, and I've spent the evening making phone calls and writing letters—letters which *will* get mailed. I already have three dates for tomorrow night."

Bailey collapsed back against the pillow and raised her arms in a silent appeal. "I was right. You're nuts. Though I suppose there *is* safety in numbers. But do they know this is going to be a group date?"

"Don't be absurd. I have them lined up in three different lounges within walking distance, an hour apart."

Bailey frowned. "I don't think you're acting wisely."

"Fine." Jodi raised one foot and inspected her scarlet toenails. "Then you know exactly how I feel about your actions."

Samantha crawled out of her nest between the pillows, looked disgustedly from one person to the other, shook herself, leaped off the bed, and stalked from the room.

Bailey and Jodi exchanged glances, then burst into laughter.

"Sometimes," Jodi said, "I don't like your dog's attitude."

Bailey went to bed, but she lay awake for a long time, staring into the darkness, cuddling Samantha close, and fighting a losing battle to keep Austin out of her thoughts. Austin the lawyer, self-possessed and competent, Austin the athlete, muscled thighs pumping as he ran beside her, but mostly Austin the lover, naked before her, flesh sweat-damp and shimmering in the moonlight, heart throbbing beneath her hand . . .

She sat up, turned her pillow over, lay back on the fresh, cool side. She had to get control of her errant emotions. But Austin's image intruded again, exciting her even in his absence.

She flipped on the lamp and reached for a book, selecting a thriller, hoping that would divert her thoughts.

The next morning as she sat in a partners' meeting for the first time, Bailey tried to regain her former excitement over that achievement. Looking at the six men gathered around the conference room table, she reminded herself that she would be the first woman partner. That was something to be proud of.

But her victory felt oddly hollow. Surely, she told herself, this lack of enthusiasm couldn't be the result of her problems with Austin. Surely she had more control than that.

She stared at the few drops of sludge left in her cup. Maybe a little more caffeine . . .

"Stafford," she said, "I'm going for more coffee before we get started here. Anyone want me to bring them some?"

Seated at the head of the table, Stafford waved his cigar at her. "Sit down. Jodi's on her way with coffee and rolls."

Good, Bailey thought, settling back into the chair. Surely caffeine and sugar would improve her mood, banish her distressing memories of the night before.

"What we're here to discuss," Stafford boomed, interrupting her thoughts, "is a merger offer from a larger firm."

That was one way to wake up, Bailey thought, accepting a copy of the offer. First you learn you're going to be a partner, then you're not sure with which firm or how far down the roll. She listened with a growing sense of horror as Stafford hit the high points, named names. Somehow it didn't surprise her that her nemesis in one area of her life was intruding into another.

"Take a couple of minutes to skim over this—you can read it in detail later—then tell me what you think," Stafford ordered.

A couple of quick knocks sounded on the door, and Jodi squeezed in, balancing a large tray holding a pot of coffee and a huge plate of sweet rolls.

"You're a lifesaver," Bailey said as Jodi set the tray in the middle of the table.

"Can I get you anything else?" she asked the room at large.

"Looks like we're set," Stafford answered, and Jodi turned and left the room.

Secretaries always served coffee, but this time Bailey felt strange about it. Jodi was her friend. Jodi was a part of any group she was a part of. Jodi didn't serve food like a waitress and then disappear.

"I think we ought to consider the offer," Hollis Montgomery, the only partner under the age of forty, announced. "That guy they sent over from St. Louis is doing some good things with that firm. They're on the move, streamlining their operation. It's a real chance for us to grow."

"I don't like it," Edmund Bradshaw, second in seniority to Stafford, droned. "We're doing all right by ourselves, been doing all right for a lot of years."

"What's wrong with doing better than all right?" Eugene Lawson queried.

"How much better do you want to do?" Milton Chandler asked. "Between our salaries, bonuses, perks, and side investments, every one worried about tax shelters, not about meeting the mortgage payments."

Bailey studied Stafford Morris' face as the debate continued. He looked uninvolved, almost bored.

He already knew what everyone would say, she realized. Six partners. That's why I was invited. To break the tie. But on which side was he counting her? She'd have to try to think about this objectively.

"What's your opinion, Stafford?" she asked, her first comment since the discussion had begun.

"I agree with everybody," he growled around his cigar, his eyes squinted against the spiraling smoke. "There's advantages and disadvantages, and which ones are important will be a personal call for all of us." Without raising his head, he blew a stream of smoke toward the ceiling. "How about you?"

She nodded slowly. "I need to think about all the ramifications."

That pretty much told her which side he was going to come down on. Stafford was comfortable where he was, big fish in a little pond, king of the mountain. Which meant he probably expected her to vote against the offer, too. Another aspect of the situation she'd have to ignore in making her decision.

"Be back here Monday morning," Stafford finally declared when Hollis Montgomery slammed his fist onto the table in response to Edmund Bradshaw's latest statement. "We'll fight some more and then take a vote."

Bailey returned to her office feeling more disoriented than she had at the beginning of the meeting in spite of the coffee and rolls. Falling into her chair, she spun it around and looked out the window at the parking lot next door. The rectangular cars sat quietly in tidy, rectangular rows.

Until recently, she'd thought her life was like that, tidy and symmetrical. Bad enough her personal life had gone down the tube with all her time and thoughts centering on Austin, but now her career, which had been proceeding on schedule, was suddenly an unknown element. And she would cast the deciding vote. That was a hell of a thing to put on somebody's shoulders who wasn't even officially a partner yet.

Leaning back in her chair, she crossed her arms and chewed on her bottom lip. Her instinct rebelled at the thought of merging with another firm. But on the other hand, maybe she'd grown into the situation here and could just as easily adjust to another. In a bigger firm, there was certainly greater potential for advancement and growth.

Not that Stafford Morris had ever tried to stop her personal expansion within the firm. They'd fought tooth and nail over a lot of things, and he had been known to pull rank on her. But in the overall picture, she had no real complaints. She'd pretty much been allowed to carve her own niche.

Conversely, stories she'd heard via the grapevine about the new and improved Kearns, Worley firm indicated the niches were carved before the insertion of attorneys. She could see that. Pushy as Austin was, he'd enjoy molding people to his specs, but she'd be damned if he'd get the chance to mold her.

Bailey kicked at the credenza behind her, spinning her chair back around to her desk. Damn! Her personal feelings were intruding on a business decision. She couldn't let that happen.

Pulling a yellow legal pad from the middle of one of the stacks on her desk, she ripped off the top pages and drew a line down the middle of the first blank sheet. On one side she wrote "Pro," on the other, "Con," and began making her lists.

She muttered an expletive as both sides rapidly filled. She didn't want this responsibility. If Stafford knew her decision could be influenced by personal factors . . . Or maybe the crafty old fox did know. That would be just like him, to stack the deck.

The pencil lead snapped, and Bailey realized she had

been pushing a hole into the paper. She tossed the paper and pencil into the midst of the mess on her desk.

This was all that blasted Austin's fault. He made the offer. Because of him, she was in this unenviable position.

Then it hit. She straightened as energy surged through her. Austin was asking for a merger, and the decision was in her hands. She was back in familiar territory, not the unexplored terrain of the night before. She could talk to him now. Grabbing the phone, she punched in a number she hadn't realized she'd memorized.

"Austin," she greeted when he came on the line.

"Bailey! Hello." His voice sounded excited on the first word, then dropped to an intimate tone on the second.

"So we may be in this thing together before long," she said, then explained that the offer had been presented that morning.

"Oh." She'd obviously taken him by surprise, but he rallied immediately. "How's it look? Have they made any decisions yet?"

"*We* won't vote until Monday. Stafford just presented it to us in a special partners' meeting this morning."

He took the bait. "Partners' meeting? Are you—I didn't think—"

"I know I can trust you to keep quiet for now. My partnership isn't official yet, but of course, I was invited to vote on something so important, especially since there were six partners. That could have resulted in a tie vote." She leaned back in her chair, propped her feet on her desk, waited.

"You're being made a partner? Bailey, that's great. When is the official announcement? We'll have to get together and celebrate." Give the devil his due, he sounded sincere. But then the full impact must have hit him. "Six partners?" He was silent for a moment. "Well, so, what do you think?"

"You know I couldn't possibly divulge that information, Austin, not even to a good friend like you. Firm loyalty and all that, but I'm sure you'll be the first to know when the decision is made. Oh, my client just walked in. I've got to run."

Bailey whirled around in her chair, laughed at the ceiling. "My point," she said softly. But even as she said it, she had to admit to herself that her exhilaration didn't derive solely from scoring one on Austin. Oddly, she felt more connected to him now than last night—and certainly more comfortable talking to him. Some of her elation slipped away, however, at the thought that she was limited to relating to him on that one level.

With a sigh she forced her attention back to the matter at hand. The rest of her happiness left as she acknowledged that the problem of making a decision was still unresolved, and Austin's involvement made it more complicated. Maybe she'd best let it ferment, let her subconscious work on it for a while. Get back to her work.

She flipped open the first file on her desk. A lease for Larry Haynes. She ought to dive into it and boobytrap the document with all sorts of loopholes he'd never notice until it was too late. Better shelve Larry Haynes until her mood changed.

The next folder opened to pictures of Candy Miller's wreck with—what was the little guy's name?—Alvin Wilson. From the looks of their cars, this wasn't the first wreck for either of them. The background scenery was nice, though. Springcreek Park, as she recalled from the file. A great park to run, though she hadn't been there in a while. Lots of trees, path marked in half miles. A good place to blow out the cobwebs, push the body till it hurt, set the mind free to work out difficult decisions.

Not to mention the park was across town from Austin's apartment. No chance of running into him and having him complicate matters even further.

Bailey chugged along the path, cursing the late afternoon heat and humidity. Though most of the track was shaded from the sun by the thick forest of trees on both sides, those same trees kept out any stray breezes. Even her sweatband was unable to keep the perspiration out of her eyes, and there was no such thing as an upper-lip band. This was not one of her better runs.

Add to that the fact that neither her mind nor her body seemed to be working quite right. Her legs felt strange and hard to control, which was a pretty good description of her mind. She'd give it another half mile, then turn around and go back. Best not to be in such a wooded area alone after dark, and the sun was getting pretty low.

A looseness on one foot caught her attention, and she looked to see her shoelace flying. It figured. Stooping beside the path, she yanked the lace tight and knotted it. Resting felt good, and she pondered turning around and going back.

A bicycle passed her as she straightened, and she glanced with idle curiosity at the rider. He looked vaguely familiar, though it was hard to tell from the rear. Short, pudgy, and wearing a baseball cap. Not anyone on her "A" list.

Drawing in a deep breath, she resolved to continue to the next half-mile marker before she headed back. With everything else, she didn't need to feel like a quitter.

Rounding the bend, she saw the man on the bicycle slowing as he neared a picnic area. Another rider swung onto the path and joined him. Even from the rear, there could be no mistaking the pink spandex and blond hair. Candy Miller. That's why the man looked familiar. Alvin Wilson, the party whose insurance company they were suing.

Ain't love grand? Bailey thought wryly. Run into somebody, wreck her car, injure her back, and find the girl of your dreams.

The next half-mile marker should be just ahead, and she'd definitely turn around there. She pounded noisily across a wooden bridge, then noticed two abandoned bicycles beside the path. A high-pitched giggle from beneath the bridge elicited a soft groan and an immediate U-turn from Bailey.

This run had been going down the tube from the first step, and it had finally reached bottom. That was all she needed, to see the evidence of a couple of adults who ought to know better making out in the middle of a park. It called to mind all too vividly the activities of another adult couple who'd briefly acted like teenagers in a yard near the park.

Bailey's feet pounded wildly down the path, her speed increasing, her heart racing. Was there some sort of cosmic conspiracy to keep Austin, with his electric eyes and electric touch, in front of her mind? She raced from the park, as though pursued by demons.

_____ NINE _____

The third time Austin drove by Bailey's condo, he finally saw her car in its assigned space under the covered parking. He smiled smugly as he parked and headed for her door, anxious to confront her face-to-face.

He had a legitimate reason to be at her door, a reason that went beyond his desire to see her and touch her again, an impersonal reason—to continue the discussion she'd started before the arrival of a mythical client when she'd hung up on him. He understood what she'd told him, her intimation that she was in control of his destiny, that they had another contest going. He could, after all, read between the lines when they were Bailey's lines.

He rang the doorbell and waited, rehearsing his script, preparing to win the day before she even knew what was going on. He could almost see her moving into position behind the door, her sleek, warm body disguised in one of those prim suits she always wore, her demeanor cool and regal. Two lawyers, dressed for battle.

"Austin, come in."

His script went right out of his head, along with any other coherent thoughts he might have had.

She wore a short, white terry cloth robe, her long legs emerging from the bottom and going on forever. Her wet hair was tousled atop her head, damp tendrils trailing onto her face. And to make matters worse, it took her several seconds to mask a look of delight at seeing him.

"I thought I'd see if Gordon was anywhere around," he mumbled, seizing on the first thing that came to mind.

"I haven't seen him. Did you check his office?"

"Ah, no. It's almost eight o'clock. Surely he's not still working." Eight o'clock and she'd obviously just showered. "Are you getting ready to go out?"

"No, I've been for a run. Would you like to come in and call Gordon's office? He's been working some long hours."

She held the door wide for him, and Samantha dashed out, plumed tail wagging in greeting. He reached down for the little dog, then straightened, his gaze scant inches from her long, long legs.

"Thanks," he choked out, sidling past her into her living room. Cradling Samantha in one hand, he went to the wall phone above the kitchen bar and punched out his home number, the only number he could remember at the moment. "No answer," he said, a misleading but not false statement.

Bailey had, meanwhile, taken a seat on one end of the sofa, tucking her legs and bare feet under her. Even if he'd been under oath, he couldn't have remembered what he'd originally planned to say to her.

"You're welcome to wait a few minutes and call him again," she invited.

He made his way to the opposite end of the sofa, facing her. That robe scarcely covered the essentials. How could she have answered the door wearing it when she had no idea who was out there? At the thought of her naked body barely hidden by the tiny garment, he squirmed uncomfortably. Samantha abandoned him with a disgusted look at his inability to remain still and moved to the middle cushion, settling down as a furry chaperone.

"So Gordon's not at home or at work?" Bailey asked.

Since Austin hadn't been checking on Gordon's whereabouts, he had no idea. "Hot day for a run," he said, electing to change the subject rather than have to lie.

She shrugged, leaning forward to stroke Samantha's head. The V-neck of the robe fell away, and he glimpsed the ivory contours of her breasts. "It was an okay run," she answered.

So distracted was he by her provocative attire that Austin almost missed the subtle changes. Her voice was different, and she tensed ever so slightly. Someone who knew her less well than he would never have noticed.

"Where'd you run?" he asked, trying to keep his thoughts on her odd reaction, and off his reaction to her.

"Springcreek Park." She kept her gaze averted from him.

Springcreek Park? Why had she gone all the way across town to run in a park that just happened to be the scene of the Miller/Wilson accident? "That's a long way from here," he said, leaning closer to study her expression.

"Do you want to try to call Gordon again?" she asked.

"Call Gordon? What for?" The words were out before he remembered his excuse for coming by.

But Bailey hadn't forgotten. Her eyes lifted boldly to his. Damn! For a minute there, he'd had control, but now he'd lost it.

Bailey exulted in her victory. She'd not only diverted him from her embarrassed thoughts, but had actually caught him. He hadn't been looking for Gordon at all. He'd come to see her.

"Would you like a drink?" she offered, gracious in her triumph. "I'll get us some sodas."

He'd had her off balance for a while, she admitted to herself as she rummaged in the refrigerator, staring at her as if he were ready to spring across the sofa and grab her, making her all too aware of her state of undress. Okay, she'd deliberately chosen not to change clothes when she'd seen him walking across the parking lot. Her attire might, she had hoped, give her the advantage. And he had been flustered, all right, but somehow she hadn't been able to capitalize on it.

Then he'd started talking about Springcreek Park, reminding her of the scene she'd almost witnessed as well as the similar scene she'd been a part of. And she'd become the flustered one.

"Would you like a glass?" she asked, offering him the cold red can.

When he shook his head, she sat back and waited for him to make the first move.

He raised his soft drink. "To your new status as a partner of Hoskins, Grier and Morris."

"My unofficial status," she corrected.

"Of course. But not for long. When it becomes official, we'll have champagne instead of soda."

They sipped their drinks and eyed each other warily, gleefully.

"Kind of a rough thing to do to a new partner, though," he said, leaning back into the corner of the sofa in pretended nonchalance. "Hitting you with such a major decision before you have time to catch your breath."

"Actually I'm flattered that they respect my opinion so much." She leaned back, too, stretched her legs out, then remembered her attire and tucked them under her. Damn! If she had the guts to wear it, why didn't she have the guts to use it to advantage?

"I'm sure, as a neophyte, you'll probably just go along with the majority." He clasped his hands behind his head and smiled.

"How simple you make things sound, assuming there *is* a majority to go along with." She returned his smile, swirled the liquid in her can. "And assuming I'm a follower."

He leaned forward, set his empty can on the coffee table, then flattened his palms on his knees, crushing the sharp creases in his dark slacks. She could almost feel the warmth from those hands, and instinctively her hands found the same position on her own knees.

"I'm sure it would be hard, though," he said, "for somebody who's just achieved a small plateau to be able to visualize the larger scope of things, to conceive of attaining more distant but vastly more satisfying goals." He moved closer, leaned toward her urgently.

"Probably as difficult as it would be for an entity interested only in self-advancement to allow for anyone else's growth in a way that didn't benefit him."

"Or her." He raised his hands to her shoulders, and she thought for a minute he was going to shake her, but he only held her very still, forcing her to look directly at him. "If everyone else wants a chance to move ahead, it's not fair for one person to hold them back."

They were almost nose to nose. She could feel his warm breath on her face, reminding her of the warm night air. Her own breath came faster.

"I guess if *everyone else* wants something, one person's vote won't be enough to stop them, will it?" she asked, struggling to remember what they were talking about.

His hands moved from her shoulders to her face, gently caressed her cheeks. "One person can frequently change the way things are supposed to go." His voice had become softer but more intense.

She braced her hands on his chest to keep from toppling forward against him, to hold him in place while they settled this. ''Not without cooperation.'' Whatever the hell it was they were trying to settle.

He was talking again, but she couldn't hear what he was saying. A great wind roared inside her head. Through a fog, she could see his lips moving, coming closer, so close she couldn't see them. Since there was no point in trying to see, she closed her eyes and raised her face.

The door slammed. ''I think he's following me!'' Jodi announced. Samantha flew out from her position between Bailey and Austin to climb over the back of the sofa, racing toward the sound of Jodi's voice.

Bailey pulled away from Austin, felt his touch leave her, drew in several deep breaths, tried to orient herself in time and space.

''Oh, crud!'' Jodi gasped. ''Excuse me, I didn't real-ize—I'll just pop into my bedroom. If somebody comes to the door, you never heard of me.''

''Jodi, wait!'' Bailey exclaimed. ''Come back here. What are you talking about? Who's following you?''

Jodi cast Austin a wary look. ''Seven o'clock,'' she answered. ''We'll discuss it later.'' She darted into her bedroom, closing the door behind her.

Her seven-o'clock date, Bailey interpreted. She glanced at Austin to see how he was reacting to Jodi's erratic behavior.

He blinked rapidly a couple of times, but not before she'd seen the remnants of a glazed expression in his eyes. He cleared his throat. ''Is Jodi okay?''

Bailey sighed. ''I doubt it. I think she's probably gone over the edge.''

''Well, I guess you'd better check on her, and we'll have to reschedule our, uh, discussion.''

Bailey nodded. And Jodi had better be in extremely dire straits to justify her exquisitely bad timing.

She closed the door behind Austin, grabbed her soda off the floor, slipped into shorts and a T-shirt, and charged into Jodi's room. "Your seven o'clock followed you home? I knew you'd get mixed up with a nut!"

"You know what they say, better a nut than a lawyer." Jodi lay stretched out on her bed with Samantha resting on her stomach. Neither of them looked unduly concerned.

Bailey sank to the floor in a cross-legged posture. "I never heard anybody say that," she argued.

"You did now. Sorry I interrupted just when you were getting close to a little activity behind closed doors instead of out in the open."

Bailey felt herself blush as Jodi giggled.

"Don't change the subject," Bailey ordered. "Who followed you home and why?"

Jodi folded her arms behind her head. "He was the oddest little guy. Balding, glasses, kind of meek, and he gushed on and on about how wonderful I am." She turned toward Bailey and frowned. "I shouldn't make fun of him. He was really kind of sad. But when I tried to leave, he grabbed my arm. Said I should come home with him and meet his mother. Shades of *Psycho*!"

"He grabbed you?" Bailey sat bolt-upright. "He physically assaulted you, then followed you home?"

"Don't come all unglued. He took my arm, released it when the waiter came over, and then I think I saw him when I left the last bar, and maybe in the parking lot here. But I wouldn't swear to it." She paused, then added, "Anyway, he's no taller than I am, so how many problems can he cause?"

Bailey groaned. "Do you want something to drink? I need a refill. This seems to be turning into a two-cola evening."

Jodi sat up, holding Samantha in her arms and swinging her feet to the floor. "I'll go with you, and we can see if Lennie's in the parking lot. By the way, you didn't ask about eight o'clock. He was terrific. Good-looking, great bod, great job—an airline pilot."

Bailey took two sodas from the refrigerator and handed Jodi one. "So what are you doing home this early if he was so great? Did he have a nine o'clock?"

"Of course not," Jodi answered, crossing the living room to the front window and peeking cautiously between the miniblinds.

Bailey curled into an armchair. "So tell me about your pilot," she invited as Jodi flopped onto the sofa.

"Pretty," Jodi answered, focusing her attention on Samantha, who quickly resumed her spot on Jodi's stomach.

"You said that already."

"Did I say he had a great bod?"

"Mmm-hmm."

"Nice guy. Bright. I'll probably go out with him again."

"But," Bailey supplied.

"Well, you couldn't exactly say the sparks flew." She rolled her head to the side and gave Bailey a sheepish grin. "When I left, I thought it was at least nine-thirty or ten, but it was only eight-thirty. Maybe it'll get better, though."

Bailey nodded. She'd come to the private conclusion that those blasted "sparks" Jodi mentioned were fickle creatures, coming of their own volition, totally uninfluenced by the decrees of mere mortals.

As though Jodi read her thoughts, her smile became impish. "But you don't seem to be having any problem with sparks. Did you shower together?"

"Certainly not!" She touched her still damp hair. "I showered before he got here. We were discussing—" She halted in midsentence. The merger, like everything else in a law firm, was considered a confidential topic. Of course, secretaries tended to know as much about the business as their bosses. Still, Jodi hadn't mentioned the subject, and she hesitated to bring it up—just in case. "We were discussing business," she finished lamely. That was a rotten deal, not being able to talk to her best friend about her problems. "I'd just come back from a run. And you'll never guess what I saw!"

She seized on the story of Candy and Alvin under the bridge with delight, recognizing a great diversion when she found one. Drawing out the tale, avoiding her personal feelings, Bailey soon had Jodi wiping tears of laughter from her eyes.

"So instead of writing letters," Bailey concluded, "maybe you should run into cars until you find Prince Charming. Or, to be totally accurate, let him run into you."

Suddenly she felt uncomfortable. From the sober look that crossed Jodi's face, she knew her friend felt the same way.

"Let him run into you," Jodi repeated, sitting upright.

"Coincidence," Bailey protested weakly, taking a deep gulp from her soft drink. This could turn into a three-cola evening.

"If you ask me, it sounds a little suspicious."

It certainly did, and Bailey would have seen it immediately if her mind hadn't been so muddled with thoughts of Austin and lust. "Innocent until proven guilty," she hedged, trying to defend her indefensible oversight.

Jodi shrugged, leaning back. "Whatever you think, but you better hope Austin doesn't get wind of it. He'd have that detective back on her in a New York minute."

And Bailey had just admitted to him that she'd gone running in Springcreek Park, the location of the accident. That tidbit would probably be enough to set off his suspicious mind. He had seemed awfully interested in the details.

"I think I'd better check it out," Bailey admitted, rubbing her neck, which had suddenly begun to ache. "But on the q.t." No need for everyone to know she'd temporarily lost her reasoning abilities, especially not with a partnership on the horizon and Austin poised for a checkmate should she make a wrong move.

Austin drove aimlessly around the city for half an hour, waiting for his hormones to subside and his brain to kick back into gear. Maybe it was just as well that Jodi had interrupted, because he'd definitely been out of control. His glands seemed to take off on their own when he was around Bailey. His glands, his temper, his common sense—his whole system went haywire in her presence.

A red light appeared out of nowhere, and he slammed on his brakes, cursing Bailey and Jodi and himself for his lack of attention. He'd blown the evening. He hadn't goaded her into revealing any information about the merger, hadn't influenced her vote in his favor, and certainly hadn't made any headway in smoothing out their strange relationship.

A horn sounded behind him, and Austin realized the light had been green for an indeterminate amount of time. He accelerated on down the street.

The only time Bailey had shown any loss of control was when he asked about her run, an odd thing to get upset about. And why had she gone all the way over to Springcreek Park? The whole thing sounded awfully suspicious. It was too dark tonight, but tomorrow evening immediately after work, he'd be at Springcreek Park. He'd find out what Bailey had gone to see.

If Bailey's life was splintering out of control in all directions, she could at least try to help her best friends get their lives straightened out. Just before lunch the next day, she marched determinedly down to Gordon's office. He was sitting, staring blankly into space, when she burst into the room.

"You look terrible!" she exclaimed.

"I wish you'd learn to be more direct, stop sugar-coating the facts," he drawled.

"I've come to drag you to lunch, and I don't want any flack about it."

"Drag away." Gordon extended his hands. "I'm not sure I can walk."

"Come on," Bailey ordered, starting out the door but turning back to be sure he was following. "Are you sick? With those bloodshot eyes and dark circles, you look like you've been on a week-long binge."

"I have. A work binge." He followed her down the hall.

Bailey shook her head. "*I* work hard, but I don't look like that. What are you really up to?" The poor man obviously needed her help getting straightened out in more ways than one.

"You've been working hard since you came here, developed immunities." Gordon punched the button to call a down elevator. "I've got a lot of catching up to do. This is only temporary, until I get my desk cleared off."

"That'll never happen. Not a feasible goal."

They entered the half-full elevator.

"I have a reason," Gordon admitted, and Bailey nodded in satisfaction. He was just about ready to confess, if she could only keep him awake through lunch.

At the deli Gordon scarfed down his sandwich and launched into his potato salad. Not only had the man not been sleeping, it would appear he hadn't been eating, either.

"All right, out with it," Bailey ordered when he swallowed the last bite.

"I'm trying to straighten up my life. Is that so terrible? Are you going to eat your slaw?"

She'd planned on it. "No. Do you want it?" She shoved the plastic dish across the table. "You always seemed perfectly happy with your life."

"Things change. And you needn't play innocent with

me, Ms. Russell. It didn't escape my attention that you were invited to join the big boys yesterday.''

"Oh." She shouldn't have been surprised. The office grapevine was very efficient.

"So," he said, smiling for the first time, "does this mean what I think it means?"

Bailey nodded, unable to restrain a wide grin.

Reaching across the table, Gordon took her hands in his. "That's wonderful! I knew you could do it! When do we celebrate?"

"When it's official, at the fiscal-year-end party." Then her smile faded, and she leaned forward. "Is that it, Gordon?" she asked, barely above a whisper. "Are you upset because we started at the same time, and you aren't a partner yet?"

Gordon loosed her hands and leaned back, still smiling. "Nah. You know I never had my eye on a partnership. But I would like to keep my job."

"I wasn't aware it was in jeopardy."

Gordon lifted an eyebrow. "When our laid-back firm merges with an aggressive, killer cobra firm, a lot of things will change."

Punching the ice in her glass with her straw, Bailey studied him for a few minutes. "I suppose Austin told you," she finally said. Though it pained her to give him the credit, the man seemed to be ubiquitous.

"Yes, he did." Gordon scraped the last bite of slaw from the container, swallowed, and smiled smugly.

"Some time ago, I'd guess, since you've been working your brains out practically since he arrived in town."

"Poor Bailey. It must be awful to be the last to know," Gordon teased. "I'm aware of how desperately you hate being last."

She leaned back and crossed her arms over her chest. "If you're so knowledgeable, then surely you're aware it's far from a done deal. Should the merger not occur, will you go back to leading a normal life?" Might as well add one more outside influence to her list, make things even more complicated.

Gordon stacked his plastic utensils and bowls in his plate and avoided Bailey's gaze. "That depends. I don't know. Probably not."

Enough was enough. She couldn't wait forever for these foolish people to recognize what was before their very eyes. "If you'd spend a little more time with Jodi and less time working or hiding notes and flowers in the park, she'd be a lot more impressed."

Gordon's mouth dropped open.

"Come on," Bailey said, pushing back her chair and standing. "Let's get to the office and you can call and ask her for a date like a regular, sane human being. And don't tell her I told you to. Take the credit for yourself. You need all the credit you can get."

Gordon took her arm as they wended their way through the tables. "I think being a partner is going to make you bossier than ever."

"Not possible. An absolute can't have a comparative form."

Austin slammed the door of his apartment behind him, grabbed an icy beer from the refrigerator, and flopped onto the sofa. He'd wasted the whole evening checking on Candy Miller, and all she'd done was go to the B&B Lounge. That was nothing new. The insurance company's bumbling detective had followed her there.

He'd sat in his car in the parking lot for thirty minutes before he gave up and came home. As he recalled from the testimony, she'd likely be in there for the rest of the evening.

What he needed to do was go in and observe her, ask a few questions. Maybe even talk to her. Buy her a drink and get into her confidence.

Right. And she's going to be eager to spill her guts to opposing counsel. Even Candy Miller wasn't that dumb.

Snatching up the remote control, he flicked on the television, drank his beer, and watched a bumbling detective don mustache and beard to spy on a suspect.

Oh, no, he thought, switching the channel. That was television, not real life, and he was a respected member of the legal community.

So who do you think is going to know? some perverse side of him argued. Not likely you'd see anyone there you knew, and if you should, how would they recognize you?

No way.

He gulped half his beer, switched back to the detective show.

Is your pride stronger than your desire to beat Bailey Russell?

His demented side had a point. Right now she seemed to be in control of every aspect of his life, and that was certainly an undesirable state of affairs. She knew something he didn't know about the Miller case. She had hinted strongly that the fate of the merger was in her hands. And, worst of all, she seemed to be in charge of his hormones. He drained the beer can. Even thinking about her was creating a physical problem. And it didn't just involve her body, desirable though said body was. Everything she did, from their contests to her performance at the deposition, excited him. He had to get a wedge in somehow, regain the upper hand.

But where did one even go to find a fake mustache?

That was no problem. Any lawyer could handle that. Tell his secretary to find one.

Add a pair of glasses—they were good enough for Superman—then a hat, maybe. A straw hat. Denim shirt open halfway to the waist. Tight jeans and a belt with a big buckle and his name on the back. Somebody else's name, that is. Cletus, maybe. No, Bubba.

He crushed the beer can and headed for the refrigerator to get another. Fun to play with the idea, but he had too much dignity to actually go through with it.

TEN

"No way am I going out in public dressed in that thing," Bailey protested as Jodi held up a black leather skirt that appeared to be made for a Barbie doll.

"It'll be shorter and tighter on you than it was on me, but that's all to the good," Jodi mused, ignoring Bailey's protestation and continuing to rummage in her closet. "Now for a blouse. Let's see, we need to show some skin."

"Oh, I don't think so." Bailey held the skirt in front of her. It was a good six inches above her knees. "This should be about maximum on the skin."

Jodi tossed a fuchsia tube top and a short teal blouse with waist ties onto her bed.

"Do you actually wear these things?" Bailey questioned.

"Of course I do, and so do lots of other women. It's very trendy." She opened a dresser drawer and pulled out a pair of black nylons. "Just the right touch," she approved. "Now come on to the bathroom so I can make you up."

"This is still in the supposition stage," Bailey balked. "I don't really think I can walk in that bar, made up like a floozy, and spy on Candy Miller."

147

Jodi folded her arms and rolled her eyes. "You said you wanted to get in that bar and find out what she's up to since there were no clues in your omnipotent files. You'll stand out like a sore thumb dressed in your own clothes."

Bailey eyed the costume dubiously.

"So make up your mind. I haven't got all night. I have to get ready for my date with the real Prince Charming."

"I told you Gordon would come through."

Jodi shrugged. "We'll see."

"He sends you a flower arrangement so big, it's obscene, and invites you to dine at the Peppercorn Duck Club; what else do you want to see?" Bailey took the stockings from Jodi and added them to the pile of clothes on the bed. "Let's do my face and then determine if I can carry off this crazy scheme of yours."

Thirty minutes later Jodi turned Bailey to the mirror to see her handiwork. Bailey gasped, peered closer, laughed. A heavily made-up face batted false eyelashes beneath curly blond hair.

"Your own mother wouldn't know you," Jodi promised.

"She wouldn't claim me, that's for sure. Where did you get this awful wig?" She touched the short curls tentatively.

Jodi leaned into the shower to turn on the water. "It's part of a Halloween costume I wore a few years ago."

"That does it. I will not go out in public dressed in a Halloween costume."

"Relax. Those clothes aren't part of the costume. The wig goes with a Shirley Temple pinafore. But you do what you please. Just get out of my bathroom so I can shower. Go try on the clothes and sit and think for a while about how badly you need this information. Then we'll talk about it while I get dressed."

An hour later Bailey was sitting on a barstool in the

dimly lit B&B Lounge, sipping a screwdriver and feeling ridiculous. In spite of Jodi's reassurance, she didn't exactly blend into the woodwork. Every man in the place had given her the once-over, and a few had made suggestive comments when she walked in.

"Hi, babe." This latest voice came from right beside her. The troops were closing in. She turned to see a bulky, bearded male on the next stool. "You sure are looking good," he said.

"Thank you," she said tentatively, unsure if it was the proper response.

It must have been. The man grinned hugely. "Haven't seen you in here before."

"I haven't been in here before." Getting picked up by King Kong wasn't part of her plan, but she didn't suppose she could afford to alienate a regular who might know Candy.

"How 'bout another one?" He indicated her drink.

"Ah, no, thanks. I'm fine. My boyfriend's due before long, and he doesn't like me to drink too much." There. That should cool him down.

"Your boyfriend, huh? Too bad."

"Say, if you come in here a lot, maybe you know a couple of my friends, Candy Miller and Alvin Wilson. I was kind of wondering if they'd be in tonight."

"Sure I know Candy and Al. She ought to be here pretty soon, but he don't come in with her since they got that car wreck thing going." The man drained whatever remained of his beer in one gulp and slammed the empty can onto the bar, causing Bailey to jump at least six inches.

"Ready for another one, Mike?" the bartender asked as he replaced the can with a full one.

Bailey's heart raced as she clutched her own drink in both hands and made a pretense of sipping. She had obtained some vital information, but where did she go from here? This wasn't quite the same thing as examining a witness in the courtroom.

"Reckon they'll still remember their old friends after they get all that money?" she finally asked, affecting a drawl.

"Shoot, yeah. Don't you remember a few years back when Candy and that other guy, Murray, I think his name was, got a big settlement on his neck after he let her run into him? His golden neck, he used to call it."

Mike guffawed, and Bailey squeezed out a smile in an effort to join him.

"No, I don't remember that," she said when Mike settled down. "Candy had just run old Murray off when I met her."

Mike laughed with his whole body this time and swigged another portion of beer. "You women," he said. "Old Murray run off and left her one fine day is what really happened, but don't you tell her I told you so."

"I won't. Don't worry. So he left her, you say? What a jerk." Bailey wrapped both hands around her glass to keep them from trembling. "Uh, that wasn't Murray Anderson, was it?"

"Nah. I think old Murray's last name was Ferritt or Ferrell—that's it. Murray Ferrell."

"Oh, yeah. I remember now." You asked for it, you got it. "Would you excuse me?"

"For what?" He looked at her quizzically.

"I need to go to the ladies' room." She had to be alone for a minute and assimilate this new information.

"Over there," he advised, pointing to a dark corner.

"Thanks." Bailey slid off the stool and tried to avoid eye contact with any of the men who looked, whistled, or made other obscene noises.

The ladies' room wasn't exactly conducive to thinking. Someone had used it for a private smoke recently, and Bailey suspected the cigarette hadn't been purchased from a vending machine. Since she didn't dare sit anywhere or even lean against one of the walls, she paced back and forth in the small room.

The evidence was overwhelming that Candy Miller was a fraud. She'd been involved in an insurance scam before.

Okay, Bailey thought, you've got the information. Now, what on earth do you do with it? Drop the case? The accused was presumed innocent until proven guilty. She hadn't really proven that Candy was perpetrating a fraud. But the circumstantial evidence was pretty incriminating.

An impatient knock sounded on the door, and the knob rattled.

"I'll be right out," Bailey called

As she strode back into the bar, the low murmurings and whistles broke into her concentration, irritated her. With her haughtiest gaze in place, she raised her head to confront the creeps and shut them up. They smiled at her, completely undaunted. And coming in the door, as luck would have it, she saw a vaguely familiar face.

She slid back onto her stool and turned to look again. The man definitely reminded her of somebody. He was attractive in a rural sort of way. "Great bod," as Jodi would say. Slim hips, dark hair bristling out of his unbuttoned shirt. As he momentarily turned away from her, she saw the name "Bubba" on the back of his belt.

"Somebody you know?" Mike asked.

"No. He looks familiar, but I'm sure I don't know anyone named Bubba."

Beside her, Mike slammed another empty beer can down. At the far end of the bar, Bubba slid onto a stool. The bartender handed Mike another beer, then moved on to the new customer. Bubba looked up at the bartender, in Bailey's general direction.

It wasn't possible, but even in the dim light and behind the glasses, she couldn't mistake those eyes.

Austin was here, which meant Austin was suspicious. He'd be even more so when he noticed her, and it wouldn't take him long to find out what she'd already found out.

But the panic that seized her dropped her just as suddenly, and Bailey relaxed for the first time since entering the bar. He'd never know she was here. All he'd see was a blond floozy. And if she looked as desirable as the men in the bar seemed to think . . .

"You know, I believe I do know that guy. Think I'll just mosey over there and see," she drawled.

Mike grinned through the tangle of his beard. "You be careful now, darlin'. Your boyfriend come in and catch you—we don't need no more fights in here."

"I think this is a business acquaintance."

Mike winked suggestively. "You never did say what kind of business you're in, sweetheart."

She was halfway around the bar before she realized what Mike meant.

"Hi, cowboy," she said to Austin, trying to keep her voice a husky whisper.

Austin almost fell off the barstool. What, in the name of all that was sacred, was Bailey doing in this bar, dressed like a hooker?

Probably the same thing you're doing, he thought, answering his own question.

"Hi, uh, sugar." Knowing his voice was the only way she could possibly recognize him, he pitched it a few octaves lower and added a drawl.

"Mind if I join you?" she asked, sliding onto the stool next to him.

"I'd be plumb delighted, little lady. I'll even buy you another drink." Austin smiled as he signaled the bartender.

What a stroke of luck! If he worked it right, she'd waste her entire evening prying bogus information out of him, then when she left, he'd get down to business and find out just what she was so interested in.

She returned his smile as she accepted the drink.

"I believe you're about the purtiest little filly I've

ever seen in here," he said, playing the role. And it was the truth in spite of the makeup and fright wig.

She tilted her head sideways and peered at him coyly. "I'll bet you've seen a lot of 'fillies' to compare me with." Her voice, always pleasantly low in pitch, was husky, overtly sexy.

Where had she come up with such a corny act? She'd obviously been watching too many movies. Well, he could play that game, too. He reached over and took her hand, pretending to examine the gaudy ring she wore. Without a word, he turned her hand over and stroked the palm, raising his eyes to hers.

She met his gaze boldly and held it while stirring her drink with her index finger, then placed the finger in her mouth and slowly sucked off the orange juice and vodka. The surf began to pound in Austin's ears. He peered closely at the woman, suddenly uncertain it really was Bailey. She couldn't possibly be acting in such a seductive manner, even with the movies for guidance.

As he ran his finger down her wrist, Austin noticed that her pulse was racing. Or maybe it was his own pulse throbbing all the way to the ends of his fingers.

He turned on his barstool to face her. She moved with him, placing her long, bare legs between his. They certainly looked like Bailey's legs. They affected him the way Bailey's legs affected him.

"That surely is a nice little skirt," he told her, molding his hands to her hips. Soft leather covering firm flesh. He squirmed on the barstool. The snug jeans were becoming painfully tight.

"I borrowed it from my roommate," she replied, running her hands over his hands, over the skirt, down her smooth thighs. "Do you think it's too short?"

"I wouldn't mind if it was a few inches shorter or—" he drew a finger across her bare midriff "—a whole lot lower."

She retrieved her drink, sipped, then slowly licked her lips.

The jukebox kicked into a country song, and Austin's eyes narrowed. This was his chance to find out if she'd lied to him that evening at Reilly's when she'd told him she couldn't dance.

With an effort of will, he withdrew his hands from her hips.

"Why don't we do a little boot-scooting, darlin'?" he asked casually.

She reached over to trail her fingers down his neck, then began toying with the top snap on his shirt. "I'm afraid that's not one of the accomplishments in my repertoire," she purred, and undid the snap. "But maybe you could teach me."

The dance floor was about the size of a first-year associate's office, but it didn't matter. Bailey had told the truth about her dancing abilities. She fell all over herself and him, too. Laughing hysterically, they stopped after only a few steps, and with a smoldering look, Austin pulled her tight against him and began to dance in place. She managed to follow that action nicely, swaying her leather-covered hips against his.

Somewhere in the back of his mind, Austin remembered this was all an act and had some sort of purpose, but he couldn't remember what, nor did he care. All he cared about was Bailey—Bailey's sleek body that fit so nicely against his, her faint, spicy scent, her ragged breathing that told him she wanted him, too. He needed to be a part of her again, to be united completely, to race together to the ultimate peak the way they had that night in Gordon's yard.

He scanned the room desperately. The jukebox was too small and close to the wall for the two of them to hide behind.

"Bailey, sweetheart," he groaned into her ear, his hands caressing her rounded buttocks, "let's go to my apartment."

She sighed and snuggled closer, and he heard himself moan.

Then she shoved him away, her eyes spitting green fire. "You knew!"

"What? What's the matter?" Austin struggled to clear the fog from his senses and fathom what was happening.

"You called me 'Bailey,' moron. I never told you my name. You knew all along, you scheming, conniving creep! You come in here in that absurd disguise and—and come on to me, and you knew it was me!" She strode angrily toward the door.

Austin followed her outside, then grabbed her arm and spun her around to face him. "Of course I knew it was you. Do you think I'd want to make love with some bimbo from a bar? You, on the other hand, seemed awfully willing to carry on with a man you'd never met!"

Bailey jerked her arm free and glared at him, her eyes deep and dangerous. "Cretin. I hate to destroy your illusions, but I recognized you the second you walked in the bar. And let's be completely clear about one thing. I wasn't carrying on with you. I was just . . ."

"What?" he asked, enjoying her sudden discomfort. "You were just what?" He grasped both her arms in case she decided to punch him, and for a brief instant, she seemed to relax. He leaned toward her, his lips parting automatically.

But she jerked free of his hold and whirled away from him. He watched her run across the parking lot toward her car, stumbling in the heels, but nevertheless presenting a most intriguing spectacle in her leather skirt.

As she drove away, he leaned against somebody's car, pulled off the hat and glasses, and considered what Bailey had just said. Setting aside the insults, she had known who he was and had flirted with him outrageously, had made it very obvious that she wanted him. Maybe she'd thought herself disguised, but her emotions had been unmasked and open. Twirling the glasses, he smiled into the night.

"Hey, aren't you that lawyer?"

Austin looked up to see Candy Miller approaching, wearing a spandex miniskirt. Everyone but Bailey, he thought, should be prohibited from wearing clothes like that.

"Yes," he answered Candy. "I'm a lawyer." Then, as he came back to earth and reality, he ground his teeth.

"See you inside, honey!" she called, opening the noisy door.

"Damn!" he cursed, throwing his hat to the ground. "Damn, damn, damn!" Bailey had done it again! There was no point in following Candy into the bar if she knew who he was.

He kicked the hat all the way back to his car.

Bailey slammed the front door behind her, threw the wig onto the dining room table, kicked her shoes across the room, turned, and kicked the wall. Samantha scuttled into the room, then tucked her tail and started to scuttle away again until Bailey held out her arms.

"I'm going to kill him," she swore, cuddling the little dog against her face. "I will kill that man in front of a dozen witnesses, and no jury in the world will convict me."

"What are you raving about?"

Bailey whirled around to see Jodi standing in her bedroom doorway, wearing a nightgown and yawning.

"What are you doing home?" Bailey asked, then blushed as the implications of the situation dawned on her. "Oh! I didn't realize—I thought—I'm just going to bed. Don't mind me." She grabbed the wig off the table and began scouting around for the shoes.

"The reason I'm here is because I got stood up. Now, what are you looking for and why are you acting so weird?" Jodi asked, coming over to join the search.

Bailey straightened. "Stood up? You mean Gordon isn't . . .?" She waved a hand in the general direction of Jodi's bedroom.

Jodi flopped onto the sofa. "No, he isn't. I neither know nor care where Gordon is. And judging from your rantings, I'd guess your evening wasn't much better than mine."

"I can't believe Gordon stood you up. There must be some mistake." Bailey sank onto the sofa beside her friend, and Samantha curled into a ball between them. The extravagant floral arrangement was conspicuously absent from the coffee table. "Where . . . ?"

"I snipped off all the flowers and put the stems on his doorstep."

"No, you didn't."

"They're in your room," Jodi confessed with a shrug. "They became suddenly offensive. Set off my hay fever."

"I'm sure there's a logical explanation," Bailey persisted.

"Right. I probably misunderstood the terms. I missed the part where he said we were going to have this date at separate places. In any event, he didn't show, which shouldn't come as a surprise to those of us familiar with the morals of lawyers. Male lawyers."

"Well, it does come as a surprise. That's not like Gordon. All the things we've done together, he's never let me down. You know how he even showed up for that race when he didn't want to." She shook her head. "No, there's more to the story."

"Right. We'll probably read in the morning paper about how he was kidnapped and held for ransom, or spent the night on an alien spaceship." Jodi stretched her arm over the back of the sofa and laid her head on it.

"Did you call his house?"

"I tried," Jodi admitted. "The first time, it rang, then it sounded like somebody lifted the receiver, but nobody said anything, just a lot of static. After that, all I got was a busy signal. The operator said there was trouble on the line. As in the phone being off the hook, for example.''

"Let's go over to his house."

"I will not!'' Jodi protested, sitting bolt-upright. "And you won't, either. Leave me a little dignity.''

Bailey threw her hands into the air. "Gordon could be lying over there dead, and you're worried about your dignity!''

"It seems to me you're being unusually dramatic about this whole thing, possibly to avoid talking about your evening and this man you're going to kill.''

Bailey cringed as the remark struck home. She was concerned about Gordon, but the whole truth was, she found his behavior easier to think about than her own.

"Austin came to the bar,'' she admitted.

"Go on,'' Jodi encouraged, settling comfortably into one corner of the sofa, facing Bailey.

"If you insist on leering like that, I won't tell you a thing. Not that there's anything to tell.'' Bailey folded her arms over her chest, then quickly unfolded them as she touched her bare midriff and remembered the way Austin had touched her.

"I can tell by the look on your face that this is going to be good,'' Jodi said. "Want me to make some hot chocolate?''

"No!'' She wasn't about to confess to the way she'd lost control, practically made love with Austin on the dance floor. "All that happened was, Austin came into the bar wearing this ridiculous cowboy outfit. I recognized him at once, of course, and went over to try to divert his attention so he wouldn't find out what I found out.'' Suddenly it hit her that she hadn't thought about her recently acquired information since Austin's appearance. His ability to distract her from the important aspects of her life was really frustrating.

She ran a hand through her hair, still sweat-damp

from wearing the stupid wig. "I found out that Candy is probably a fraud. She's been involved in another personal injury suit with another man. I got his name, and I'll check out the details on Monday, but I have an eerie feeling they're going to be similar."

"Oh, boy." Jodi grimaced. "Austin's going to love it when you have to throw in the towel because your client's a fraud."

Bailey nodded dismally. "I think I diverted him tonight, but he'll find out eventually. Maybe he's known all along. Maybe that's why he got involved in the suit. No, that doesn't compute. If he'd known, he wouldn't have offered a settlement."

"A lot of companies settle to avoid the expense of going to court," Jodi pointed out.

"Not Austin. He'd fight to the bitter end. He'd never compromise." Bailey smiled, then quickly turned it into a frown. That hadn't come out right.

Not surprisingly, her irritating friend hadn't missed it. "You sound proud when you say that." Jodi tilted her head to one side and smirked. There was no other word for her expression. "Tell me how you diverted him tonight."

"Would you look at the time? I'd better get to bed." She scooped Samantha into her arms.

Jodi's laughter followed her even after she closed her bedroom door. Let her laugh, Bailey decided. She'd laugh even louder—not to mention smirk—if she knew the whole story.

Bailey felt incredibly foolish about the way she'd acted. The events of the evening would certainly not go down as a point on her side of the tally sheet. She'd made a perfect idiot of herself. And the really awful thing was, she'd loved every minute of it, had been able to turn loose of her inhibitions and become thoroughly immersed in the erotic overtures she was giving as well as receiving. Worse yet, a part of her regretted her sudden departure, wished Austin hadn't called her by name, that he'd gone on holding her all night, that they could have gone to his apartment and made love again.

Even though it was Saturday, when Gordon hadn't shown up at the office by noon the next day and his answering machine was picking up his calls, Bailey started to get worried. When she arrived home and opened the door, however, she was not so distracted that she failed to notice the huge lavender teddy bear occupying an armchair, apparently watching television. Samantha's shaggy head peeped over one of the stuffed legs. Her tail appeared in the air, waving furiously, but she seemed disinclined to leave her comfortable nest.

"Do come in, if you can find room," Jodi invited, switching off the television and turning her head to peer over the back of the sofa. "This—" she swept an arm around the room—"has been going on since ten-thirty, when the candy arrived."

A large, golden box of Godiva chocolates sat on the coffee table, along with a porcelain music box featuring a little boy holding his hat in his hands, eyes pitifully downcast, a jigsaw puzzle with a castle in the clouds beneath a rainbow, and a basket of sloppily dyed Easter eggs, each with one wax letter, together spelling out "I'm sory."

"What a lousy speller," Bailey observed.

"I ate the other *r* for breakfast," Jodi explained. "Help yourself if you're hungry."

"You have the soul of a Mongol." Bailey sank to the floor in front of the teddy bear and scratched Samantha's ears. "So the prince is charming again and all's right with the world."

Jodi leaned over, removed the lid from the chocolates, and selected a piece from the half-empty top layer. "Help yourself," she invited. "If eating them won't offend your soul."

"Well, it's not quite like eating the Easter eggs." Bailey took a couple of the rich candies.

Jodi licked her lips and her fingers. "The jerk has good taste, but no, he isn't charming, and all isn't right with the world. I assume your friend has been sending these things—" she spread her arms "—but I haven't heard a word of explanation or apology."

"Don't forget the eggs," Bailey pointed out. "That was an apology before you ate part of it."

"Not counting the stupid, motley eggs."

The doorbell rang.

"Can you think of anything he's forgotten?" Jodi asked.

Bailey shrugged. "Want me to get it?"

"Nah. The delivery boy and I are becoming good friends. I think he's just about ready to ask me to his prom."

Bailey didn't see anyone when Jodi opened the door, but she heard Jodi say, "This isn't funny," then burst into contradictory laughter.

Standing to get a better view, Bailey could see Gordon's golden head as he knelt just outside the door. "I fell asleep," he said, rising and offering Jodi a paper crown from a fast-food chain balanced on one of his sofa pillows. "I was just going to catch a quick catnap. When I woke up, it was nine o'clock. I started to call you to apologize for being late and noticed the phone lying on my pillow. I guess it rang, and I took it off the hook without waking up, then just snored into the receiver. Anyway, then I realized the sun was shining in my bedroom window, and even with daylight saving time, the sun doesn't shine at nine in the evening. I knew I was in trouble."

Jodi motioned him inside and closed the door. "Bailey's neighbors don't need to know she associates with madmen," she explained, crossing her arms and looking defiantly up at him.

"Tell her how exhausted I've been, how I've been working myself to a frazzle," he appealed to Bailey.

"He's definitely frazzled," Bailey agreed, trying to stifle her own laughter.

"I believe you," Jodi said. "If you were making it up, surely you could do better than that."

"I considered it," Gordon admitted, "but I didn't think you'd believe judges held court twenty-four hours a day and sequestered attorneys or that I'd been in the emergency room at the hospital all night if I showed up with no cuts or bruises."

"Good thinking."

"You believe me? Can I put this down?" When Jodi inclined her head, he set the cushion on the dining room table. "And everything's all right." He sounded a little dubious. Jodi hadn't moved, didn't appear to be giving him much feedback. "And we can carry on even if it is a few hours later."

"What, exactly, did you have in mind?"

"I can get these great box seats at the Woodlands. How about we go watch the ponies run, then maybe some Italian food? I know this place in Westport—"

"On one condition." Bailey didn't like the expression on Jodi's face, a cross between a smirk and a sneer.

Gordon held one hand over his heart and raised the other. "I promise not to leave your sight the entire evening. If I fall asleep, you can just reach over and tap me on the shoulder."

"Bailey and Austin have to go with us."

"No problem," Gordon agreed.

"No way!" Bailey exclaimed so vehemently, Samantha opened one eye and glared at her.

ELEVEN

Austin was studying his photographs, contemplating exactly when and how he should spring his latest triumph on Bailey, when Gordon phoned.

"Going to the Woodlands sounds like a super idea," Austin agreed, though the "super" part had nothing to do with horses. After last night at the B&B Lounge, he couldn't wait to see Bailey again, and Gordon's offer provided him with the perfect excuse. Now that he'd seen her feelings "unmasked," she couldn't again retreat into her glacial persona.

Not to mention that he'd also have the perfect opportunity to drop little hints all afternoon, have her on pins and needles wondering how much he knew about Candy Miller, then save the real surprise for later, maybe even for the trial. Facing Bailey across a courtroom should be a real experience.

He looked at the series of photographs one more time before going in to shower and change clothes. The pictures weren't what he'd expected, but in a way they were even better.

The scam he'd tried to work was an old one, and he'd been a little ashamed of himself for not coming up with something better. But after the fiasco at the bar, he had to do something. So he bought a case of inexpensive wine, taped a bow to the top, and took it to Candy Miller's house early Saturday morning. Leaving it in Candy's front yard beside her newspaper, he parked down the street with his camera equipped with a telescopic lens and waited. And waited. Candy was not an early riser.

Finally, shortly after ten o'clock, when Austin's boredom had reached major proportions and his legs were numb from sitting, Candy appeared. Wearing a magenta robe, hair shooting out in irregular spikes, she staggered through the doorway and scanned the yard. Catching sight of the box, she approached it warily, and Austin readied his camera, hoping for a good shot of her lifting the heavy carton, a difficult task for someone with an injured back. But he was disappointed. Snatching up the newspaper, she tottered back into the house.

Austin lowered the camera. Maybe he should have opted for something not quite so heavy. If she brought out a dolly to carry it on, he'd just be out one case of wine, and Bailey would still have the upper hand.

Then his lips curved upward in a smile and he began snapping away as Candy reemerged from the house with Alvin Wilson in his bathrobe. He lugged the box inside while she tripped along beside him, her lips moving in apparent animated conversation.

And Austin captured it on film for posterity.

The photo development place didn't deliver within the advertised hour, but close enough. Austin had the evidence in his hands, and he couldn't wait to confront Bailey. Now the only thing was to figure out how to go about it in the best possible way, a way calculated to let her know he'd won this one.

Austin hummed as he slapped on a little extra cologne. This should be a real surprise. Though he was pretty sure Bailey knew something wasn't right with her client, he couldn't believe she knew the full extent of the woman's duplicity. However pushy and argumentative she might be, he didn't doubt her integrity for a minute. If she knew Candy Miller was a fraud, she'd never represent the woman.

Of course, he couldn't be one hundred percent positive about Candy Miller. There was no law against having an affair with your opponent. But it would create a lot of doubt in the minds of a jury.

He smiled at his image in the mirror. This could be quite a battle, and he had some great ideas about how they could celebrate when it was all over, how he would light sparks in those cool, green eyes.

Half an hour later he knocked on her door, knowing Bailey well enough to be prepared for anything. She didn't disappoint him. Smiling warmly, she shook his hand and welcomed him as a long-lost friend. She didn't say much on the drive to the track, but that could have been because it took Jodi and Gordon most of the trip to make a coherent tale of a purple teddy bear.

However, they had barely settled into their box seats at the track when Bailey stood and took his arm. "Let's go get some cold drinks," she urged. "Jodi, Gordon, soda or beer?"

"You stay here, Bailey. I'll go with Austin," Gordon offered, starting to rise, but Bailey gently pushed him back down as her grip on Austin's arm tightened.

"That's okay. Austin and I have something we need to talk about."

At least they were in agreement about that. He gladly accompanied her to the refreshment stand.

As they took their place in line, she turned to him. "Gordon and Jodi need some time alone," she said. "They're having problems."

"So I gathered from the teddy bear tale," he agreed.

"We also need to pretend to get along when we're around them. Do you think you can do that? Just for the day?"

Her tone irritated him. He'd thought they *were* getting along. As usual, she'd managed to arouse him in one way or another.

"I can if you can," he snapped, then, when she glared at him, he placed an arm around her shoulders and smiled through gritted teeth. "Of course I can." Seeing the concern for their friends so evident on her face and feeling her slim shoulders beneath his arm, he almost believed he could.

After delivering the drinks, they went downstairs together, ostensibly to watch the horses and jockeys when they warmed up.

"Look at the sleek muscles on number five," she said, pointing to the animal he had just been admiring.

Her words brought his attention to the sleek muscles outlined by her tight blue jeans. "The jockey's overweight," he grumbled, irritated at the line his thoughts had so easily taken when she'd resumed her cool aloofness. Then he remembered his promise of only a few minutes before. "But it is a beautiful animal. What do you think about number two? His trainer's racked up a pretty impressive record of wins."

She looked at him in surprise. "Come here a lot, do you?"

Austin leaned against the rail, enjoying his advantage. He had the edge on her now. Then, with a shrug, he tossed it away. "I have a friend in St. Louis," he said. "He owns a horse and loves to talk."

She nodded slowly, turned back to the horses and studied them for a moment, then moved a few inches closer to him. "I think two looks tired today. Do you think the trainer's record is good enough to compensate for that?"

It wasn't possible. Bailey hadn't really asked for his advice. He looked at the horse, trying to see what she saw. The animal looked fine to him. "Why do you think he looks tired?" he finally asked.

"*She* just seems a little off her stride. Look at her gait."

Austin looked. He didn't see anything wrong. "Studied a lot of horses' gaits, have you?" he asked, mimicking her earlier question.

She leaned on the rail, watching the animals. "A few. You're forgetting I grew up in a small town, surrounded by farms. I've seen a few horses in my lifetime."

He digested the information for a moment. "So which ones look good?"

Bailey couldn't believe it. Austin was actually asking her opinion about something. Not only was that a first for him, but it seemed somehow to negate the foolish image she'd projected the night before. Some of the tension left her shoulders and neck.

She studied the animals intently, looking for sleek muscles, easy gaits, the tilt of a head, the indefinables that said a horse or a human would be a fast runner, a determined competitor.

As they stood together at the rail, Austin casually draped his arm over her shoulders, sending her pulse on a race of its own. She had to admit, he had a way of generating excitement even when they weren't fighting. Taking a deep breath, she forced herself to act as unconcerned as he.

She suggested a couple of horses, and Austin held the racing form so they could both study it. Leaning his head close to hers, he discussed jockeys, trainers, records, and other variables.

"Okay," he finally said. "My money's on number nine."

When she agreed, they started back inside to place their bets. His arm dropped to her waist, and she was puzzled to find his touch not only unbearably exciting, but comfortable at the same time. Had her embarrassment been so great the night before that nothing would bother her now? Or maybe, having survived the situation, having seen each other at their worst, they no longer had a need for constraint. In any event, she moved closer to him.

When they returned to the box, Jodi looked up. "Who've you got?" she asked.

"Nine," Bailey answered, settling into a chair. "Surprise Finish. What about you?"

"Prince Charming. How could I resist? What's your choice, Austin?"

"Nine," he replied, sitting next to Bailey, taking her hand, and smiling conspiratorily.

From the corner of her eye, she caught the exchange of astonished glances between Jodi and Gordon.

"You both chose the same horse?" Jodi asked in amazement.

This was almost as much fun as beating Austin at something.

When Surprise Finish came in first, Jodi jumped to her feet. "You won!" she exclaimed, clapping.

"Umm-hmm," Bailey agreed, restraining her own excitement, trying to act as though there had never been a doubt in her mind.

"Beginner's luck," Gordon assured Jodi, tearing up his ticket and tossing the confetti into the air. "They don't have a great system like you do. Who do you like in the second?"

"As a matter of fact, we do have a system," Austin said, standing and looking smug. "Shall we go talk directly to the horses again, partner?" He extended an arm, and Bailey took it, smiling up at him as they strolled away.

Since, Bailey and Austin maintained, ill-gotten gains had to be spent right away, they treated Jodi and Gordon to dinner with their winnings acquired from a large percentage of the races.

"Well," Gordon drawled as they strolled across the

parking lot to his car, "how about we all go by my place for an after-dinner drink?"

The afternoon and evening had been wonderful, and Bailey really didn't want it to end. However, the way Gordon and Jodi looked as they walked hand in hand, gazing at each other with silly grins on their faces, told her they would probably just as soon have that drink alone.

"It's been a long day," she said.

"Yes, it has. I'm beat," Austin added.

Though he was only agreeing with her, Bailey didn't want him to want the day to end. She cast a surreptitious glance at him, but could tell nothing from his expression.

"Would you mind dropping us by Bailey's place so I can get my car?" Austin asked.

"No problem," Gordon replied.

Well, Bailey thought, examining the data, Austin had said, "dropping *us*," but then he'd referred to getting his car. The evidence concerning the end of the evening was inconclusive.

Gordon drove to her condo and let them out. Austin stood beside her in the parking lot and waved as Gordon and Jodi drove away.

"We really had them going," he said, taking her hand as they strolled down the sidewalk and up the stairs to her door.

"I think Jodi gave serious consideration to the idea we really were talking to the horses!" Bailey agreed, unlocking the door, then reaching down to catch Samantha as she dashed out.

"They'd never believe the truth if we told them."

They looked at each other and burst into laughter. As the laughter faded and neither of them moved, Bailey wanted to ask what "the truth" really was. Instead she stepped inside the doorway.

"I appreciate your cooperation tonight," she said, and hoped he'd deny that was "the truth" of which he'd spoken, that cooperation wasn't the only thing that had happened that evening.

He did. Following her inside, he closed the door behind them, took Samantha from her, and set the little dog on the floor. Wrapping his arms around her, he gently drew her to him, and somehow her own arms naturally made their way about his neck.

He smiled and shook his head in amazement. She understood. That was the way she felt.

His lips as they touched hers were familiar and strange. They'd kissed before, but never so easily—never deliberately. The burst of flame she always felt when Austin touched her was still there, but a warm intimacy now surrounded it.

He moved back from her a few inches and gazed at her through slitted, smoky eyes. A slow smile curved his lips.

"You're so . . ." he began, then the smile widened, and he traced one finger down her cheek. "You're so . . . Bailey." Bending toward her, he claimed her lips again, moving, caressing, then sliding away, trailing down her throat. With a soft groan, he pressed her to him tightly.

The flames already igniting every inch of her body, especially those inches Austin was touching, blazed higher. She sighed, reveling in the exquisite feelings. Maybe they could stay like this forever. At least until the morning when she'd have to feed Samantha.

But his warm mouth was moving onward, downward, eliciting new, wonderful sensations, igniting fires that demanded ever more fuel. He slipped the top button of her blouse and pushed aside the fabric, and she wasn't sure if the heat arose from his kisses or directly from her breast. Boldly, brazenly, she tangled her fingers in his thick hair, urged him on, though he didn't seem to need any urging.

As he fumbled with the other buttons of her blouse, his gaze returned to hers. In his eyes she saw the same overpowering desire she'd seen the night on Gordon's lawn, but now there was something else. Amid the leaping blue flames a softness smoldered, demanding and offering.

Then her blouse slid off her shoulders, and he pressed her closer, his lips returning to hers with that same odd mixture of passion and tenderness. A moan started in her midsection and rose from her throat into his mouth as she opened to him, tasted wine and peppermint candy, felt his moist warmness, the smoothness of his mouth, and the roughness of his tongue.

Frantically she unbuttoned his shirt, pressed her bare breasts against the coarse hairs and hard muscles of his chest, and it was his turn to moan. His fingers trembled as he fumbled with the clasp of her jeans, and that trembling increased her passion, overwhelmed any inhibitions she might have had left. Their desires moved together as surely as their psyches had been together all evening.

His mouth again left hers, moved down to her breast, seeking and finding first one turgid peak, then the other. She leaned against the door for support, her legs and knees suddenly weak.

As if sharing the same mind, they sank to the floor together, and he slid her jeans down her hips, then tossed them aside with his own. For a moment she leaned away from him to look, to capture his naked body in her memory, to see and incorporate every muscle, every hair, every inch of him.

With one hand he traced a gentle line down her cheek and neck, over her breast and stomach, down the valley of her waist and over the curve of her hips. She looked at him, and again it seemed her thoughts were joined with his. In his eyes she saw a reflection of the need she felt to enfold and encompass him.

Then his flesh was against hers, joining with her, and the need was met. They moved in perfect unison instinctively, and she was almost unable to endure the exquisite agony, wanting culmination but wanting it to continue forever, to be always united like this.

As their movements quickened and their passions surged to a peak, she sought his gaze, found him looking at her, and they spiraled together, bodies and souls merging in a crashing crescendo.

For a long time they remained motionless, silent, still joined. Bailey couldn't think of anything to say and felt no need to say anything. Their bodies had said it all. She was content to drift in the afterglow.

Abruptly a cold, wet nose on her cheek interrupted her mellow mood, and Bailey laughed.

Austin jerked upward, apparently as startled by her laughter as she had been by the little dog's intrusion.

"Samantha," he said when he saw the problem, "your timing is terrible."

"No," Bailey disagreed, "it could have been worse."

He grinned. "It could have been." He stood, pulling her with him and against him. "You know, she's a really short dog, much shorter than the average bed. Maybe if we found yours, we could hide up there."

His hands cupped her derrière, held her against him.

"We could try that," she murmured, and decided not to tell him Samantha regularly jumped onto her bed.

Bailey flipped the quarter for the twentieth time, recording the results on a yellow legal pad. Ten heads, ten tails. This method of eleventh-hour decision making about the merger wasn't working out any better than the more logical ones she'd tried.

The situation was bad enough of itself, but she was having a difficult time concentrating this morning. Austin hadn't left Sunday until shortly after noon. They'd made love most of the night, neither willing to admit to being tired, then gone out to brunch, but as soon as she was alone, Bailey had fallen into an exhausted sleep, waking to the morning and the miserable merger decision.

As she flipped for the twenty-first time, the time she promised herself would be the final tie breaker, Stafford Morris charged in, descended into one of her chairs, and propped his feet on her desk.

"Good morning," she snapped. "Come in. Have a seat. Put your feet up. Make yourself comfortable."

He sipped coffee from a large, thick mug, then pulled a cigar from his shirt pocket and started to unwrap it.

"You light that in here, and I'll put it out in the exact center of your head," she warned.

"Better have some more coffee," he advised. "You need it." But he returned the cigar to his pocket. "Tough decision? I thought you'd really latch on to the idea of being in control of everyone's fate."

"Just keep it up, and I'll vote against you." Bailey snatched up her mug and drained it even though the coffee was stone-cold and pretty awful.

"So you're planning to vote with me. I thought as much. You like the status quo." He looked so smug, she thought of retrieving the cigar, lighting it, and carrying out her threat.

"Which doesn't mean I have the right to vote to keep it. What about other people's rights? What if this is the wrong decision? I don't *want* to control the fate of others."

Stafford lowered his feet to the floor with a thud and stood up, grinning. "Bailey, you take things too seriously. Vote the way you want to and make it a tie vote. *I'll* break the tie."

"Not if I vote in favor, you won't," she retorted, springing from her chair and leaning toward him.

"Okay." He shrugged. "In that case, Hollis'll cast the deciding vote." Unwrapping his cigar, he left her office.

Typical irrational lawyer logic, Bailey thought, flopping back into her chair. Something you'd use to sway a jury.

She tossed the coin into the air again, slapping her hand on it as it landed, but not looking to see which side was up. Stafford's logic did make a kind of sense. At least, if you wanted to buy into it, it did. And boy, did she ever want to buy into it.

She rose, smoothed her navy skirt, and straightened her shoulders. He was right about some things, though. She did like the status quo, the small size of the firm, the familiar clients, even the incomprehensible way Stafford Morris chose to run things. And she could only cast her vote the way she felt was right, even if part of that "rightness" came from personal things like concern for Gordon's place in a big firm.

Having made her decision, she started confidently down the hall toward the conference room, but was struck midway by a strange feeling she couldn't readily identify. After a few confused moments, she admitted it was concern for Austin. This was someone's career she was voting on, not a game or a contest, and winning didn't feel like winning anymore.

With an odd rush of elation, she hurried on to the meeting. If she was concerned about Austin, that meant he wasn't influencing her vote. She wouldn't be voting against him, only against the merger. Perversely, that made it okay.

True to his word, Stafford withheld his ballot until last. However, to Bailey's surprise, the final tally showed only two votes in favor and five against.

"Feel better?" Stafford boomed as he caught up with her striding down the hall after the meeting.

"Maybe, maybe not," Bailey evaded. "If I were one of the two dissenting votes, probably not."

"You weren't," he declared confidently.

"You sound awfully sure of yourself." She turned in to her office door.

He laughed and waved his cigar as he strode away from her down the hall.

"Wait," she called, hurrying after him. "Did you know all along that someone had changed his vote?"

"Maybe, maybe not," he mocked her. "If someone did change his vote, it might be because somebody else talked some sense into him."

She followed him into his office and closed the door. "But you let me keep on worrying!"

Stafford settled in his chair behind his desk and pulled some papers in front of him. "You voted for what you wanted. That's all that mattered. All that ever mattered. Now get out of my office. I have work to do."

Bailey flopped into one of his chairs, settled her feet on his desktop, and crossed her ankles. Stafford glared at her, but she glared back.

"I have a problem—the firm has a problem—and, as managing partner, it becomes your problem." She told him what she had discovered about Candy Miller, omitting the more interesting details of how she uncovered the information. "It seems to me," she concluded, "that the firm has some potential liability."

Stafford shook his head and crushed his cigar to splinters in the ashtray. "I don't see how you got mixed up in this thing in the first place. That case was assigned to . . . uh . . ."

"Margaret," Bailey supplied.

"Yeah, her. So I don't know what you're doing anyway."

"Helping her," Bailey responded quickly.

He gave her a suspicious look. "Whatever," he finally said. "Tell Margaret to find out what's going on ASAP, and you get out of it just as fast."

For once, Bailey didn't feel inclined to argue.

Nevertheless, she soon decided she couldn't follow Stafford's orders. When she went immediately to Margaret's office and tried to explain the situation, the girl's small eyes seemed to retreat back into her round face.

"What are you trying to do?" Margaret asked. "At first you acted like you wanted to help me. Now you want to mess up the whole deal."

Bailey stood just inside the closed door of Margaret's cubicle with her arms folded, glad she hadn't elected to take a seat. It looked like she was going to have to intimidate. "This doesn't involve 'messing up a deal.' This involves a possibility—a probability—of fraud. This involves ethics, not to mention our firm's reputation."

"Everything's going great," Margaret protested. "We're probably going to win. Why are you doing this to me? You don't even know for sure that something's wrong."

"And I'm not suggesting we do anything about it until we are sure, but I *am* saying we need to look into this immediately. This is an order from the top, Margaret." If logic didn't penetrate the dense layers, maybe force would.

"Okay," the girl agreed with a shrug, averting her eyes. "I'll go check it out as soon as I get a chance."

Which evasive reply certainly, Bailey felt, justified her trip to the courthouse to determine the truth for herself, no matter what Stafford Morris said.

Austin knew he was in real trouble when he was disappointed to find that Candy Miller had been involved in another, very similar lawsuit a couple of years before. He walked down the courthouse hallway, clutching his copies of the incriminating papers, wondering exactly what he should do next. He should be thrilled to have more ammunition against Bailey, but he wasn't.

He'd thought a lot about her since leaving her Sunday afternoon and had come to a conclusion. It was vitally important to him to establish a relationship with her.

All other women were pale ghosts beside her. She made him feel vital and alive. Their lovemaking had been earthshaking, opened totally new dimensions. But he knew the weekend had been a respite. For a little while they'd touched the possibilities, but they still had a way to go before they achieved an ongoing relationship.

It represented his biggest challenge to date, but he had no doubt it would be well worth the effort.

He paused to lean over a water fountain, not really thirsty but reluctant to leave the courthouse, as though taking the information from the premises would make it real, inescapable. When he straightened, he saw Bailey heading down the hallway he'd just come up. He watched until she turned in to the doorway he'd recently vacated.

No need to speculate about what she was doing. She hadn't known the details. She was there to check and verify, just as he had been. And now, being the moral person—woman—she was, she'd admit her error and back out of the case. Which meant he wouldn't have to crush her. That would undoubtedly make their relationship a little smoother.

With a sigh he jabbed the elevator button. Which also meant he wouldn't be facing her in the courtroom. What a battle that would have been! Too bad, really. But some things had to be sacrificed.

He'd be magnanimous when she admitted defeat, comfort her. No, scratch that. Even in his fantasies, he couldn't imagine being allowed to comfort her.

He stepped into the elevator smiling so broadly, a couple of people even returned his smile.

Definitely not comfort her. Not even in defeat. Run from her, maybe! But not too fast. Let her catch him. Then when they worked up a good head of steam fighting . . .

The elevator opened and he sauntered out of the building, headed for his office.

It had taken him quite a while to dig out the information, but she would likely have more of a lead as to where to look than he did. He'd give her an hour, then phone her at the office and make dinner plans. Something simple but elegant. Maybe fish or steak. No sauces. Nothing messy in case she decided to throw it.

TWELVE

"Since you're the official attorney of record, you need to sign this and get it to the court as soon as possible." Bailey slapped a file onto Margaret's desk. The pleading paper-clipped to the front of the folder was partially hidden by a handwritten memo, "Margaret, handle ASAP."

Margaret scowled as she pulled the file across her desk, lifted the memo, and scanned the pleading.

"I checked at the courthouse," Bailey went on, "and confirmed my suspicions. Our client is trying to perpetrate an insurance fraud. She's done it before, with the roles reversed."

"So you took it upon yourself to draw up a 'Motion to Withdraw as Attorney of Record.' You don't have the right to do this!" Margaret exclaimed, pushing the file with its attachment away from her. "This isn't your case."

Bailey folded her arms adamantly. She'd expected protests after their last conversation. "Every case in this office concerns every lawyer who's a part of the firm. Since I became involved in this matter *with your approval*, and since I'm the one with the crucial information, I feel my actions are appropriate."

179

"Fine, you just go on and feel that way, and I'll take care of *my* case." Margaret drew the folder back proprietarily.

"Very well." Bailey offered a single sheet of paper covered with her sprawling handwriting. "Then you'll doubtless want to take a look at this—my notes from the courthouse."

Margaret snatched the paper eagerly, glanced at it, then scowled. "It's a photocopy."

"Yes." Bailey smiled without mirth as she turned to leave. "I have the original in case you lose that one." She paused in the doorway. "I'll be back to pick up the signed Motion as soon as you've had time to study the facts."

With a great deal of effort, she refrained from slamming the door on her way out.

When Austin got back to his office, his secretary handed him a message that Stafford Morris had called. The merger, of course. With everything else that had been happening, he'd forgotten all about that.

Easing into his chair, he studied the message slip fixedly as though he could somehow find an answer in the printed form. Bailey had hinted so strongly that she could block the deal, but would she, particularly after Saturday night?

He smiled at the memory of the easy camaraderie at the race track. His whole body tingled as he recalled the soaring vibrancy of their lovemaking, and he reached for the phone.

Having made an appointment to meet with Morris that afternoon, he decided to wait until then and approach Bailey in person about dinner. Whistling softly, he turned to work.

When he popped into Bailey's office without warning that afternoon, she seemed to be in a foul mood, barking instructions to her secretary. However, he felt a warm glow inside when she looked up at his greeting, and her scowl turned into a smile that curved her soft lips and twinkled in her sea green eyes.

"Thank you, Sharon," she said to her secretary. "We'll finish up later. Come on in, Austin. How about some coffee?"

"Can't," he replied, returning her smile, savoring her presence and her obvious pleasure at seeing him. "Got an appointment with the big guy. Maybe you could work me in for ten minutes after he's through with me."

Her smile faded slowly as he spoke. She picked up a file from her desk and looked at it, then laid it back down. "Sure," she said. A shadow settled in her usually translucent eyes.

"Great," he replied, not understanding her change. "Great. We can discuss our favorite case, new developments, uh, you know. . . ." His voice trailed off as her entire face glazed over in ice.

"If you wish to meet with me on behalf of your client, contact my secretary and we'll schedule a conference."

Jeez, she was touchy! "That's not what I meant," he said placatingly. "I'd like to talk to you about some—" he lowered his voice "—other things. I just thought maybe you and I also have something to discuss about Candy and Alvin's *activities*."

He'd been ready to deal with some anger on her part when she found out she'd lost, but not this withdrawal, this twenty-degree drop in the temperature of the room. He'd expected—even anticipated—sparks and fire.

"Bailey," came an irritated voice from the doorway, "this Candy Miller deal—oh!"

Austin turned to see the rabbity-looking associate he remembered from the insurance company's deposition glaring at him from behind her thick lenses.

"Let me get back to you on that, Margaret," Bailey responded, icicles dripping from every word.

"That's okay," Austin said. "I need to get on to

my appointment.'' He pushed past Margaret and moved into the hallway.

He wasn't eavesdropping, he assured himself, but his slow footsteps were probably a direct cause of his overhearing Margaret's angry comment just before she closed the door.

''I took it to Stafford. We can't just—'' The door slammed.

Austin's steps became slower, but his mind raced. It would seem that Bailey had no intention of admitting that her client was in the wrong. That knowledge hit hard. He'd expected more from Bailey—lots more. Never, no matter how angry he'd become with her, had he ever entertained the slightest doubt about her integrity. But even that associate knew Bailey wasn't acting ethically.

''Well, if it's not Jimmy the Greek,'' Jodi greeted him with a big grin as he approached her cubicle.

''Hello, Jodi,'' he replied, trying to pull out of his reverie and sound friendly, although small talk wasn't even a possibility considering the big things that were racing through his head. ''I think your boss is expecting me.''

She nodded and picked up the phone to announce his presence. ''How about a cup of coffee?'' she asked, ushering him into the corner office. ''It's really concentrated this time of day. A few sips are all it takes. All you can take, too.''

''No, thanks.'' He needed a drink, all right, but coffee wouldn't cut it.

When Stafford told him the merger had been voted down, he found he wasn't even surprised. Somewhere inside he'd known from Bailey's reaction to his appointment with Stafford. Through a haze, he watched the man's lips moving and heard some of the conciliatory phrases—''admire what you're doing,'' ''recommend clients we can't handle,'' ''just not right for us.'' He studied the long ash on the cigar Stafford waved around and tried to deal with his new knowledge of Bailey, a deceitful Bailey.

In hypnotic fascination, he watched the cigar ash drop onto a pleading clipped to the front of a file folder. Stafford brushed it away with no break in his discourse, but Austin's gaze remained riveted to the file. On the top left corner, a piece of notepaper printed with the words FROM THE DESK OF BAILEY RUSSELL partially covered the name of the case, but he saw enough to know it was a new pleading in the Service Insurance/Miller case. On the notepaper was the handwritten message in Bailey's unmistakable scrawl, "Margaret, handle ASAP." Bailey was pursuing the case when she *knew* her client's claim was fraudulent.

Austin realized Stafford had stopped talking. Turning his attention back to the man, Austin felt something freeze in his chest. The room took on a crystal clarity, every detail distinct. He could count the hairs on Stafford's head.

"I'm sorry to hear that," Austin said, responding to the comments about the merger. "Just for my edification, how close was the vote?"

Stafford chuckled quietly, complacently, Austin thought. "Can't tell you that. Doesn't really matter. Majority rules, one or seven."

And that, Austin thought, told him what he needed to know. Bailey had been included in the voting to make seven, and the majority had probably been by one vote. She had beaten him. Simply for the thrill of winning, she had sabotaged his efforts, his career, and was assisting in defrauding his client. She knew what she was doing was wrong. That's why she'd been so cold to him a few minutes ago.

Somehow Austin managed to stand, smile, and shake hands with Stafford. Jodi's mouth was moving as he walked past her, but he couldn't hear the words over the roaring in his head.

Bailey's door was open. When he charged in, she

stood, her ivory skin becoming even paler, her eyes huge.

"I had to do what I felt was right," she said quietly, her voice strangely calm considering the circumstances.

"Right?" he stormed. "All you want to do is win. 'Right' isn't even part of your vocabulary."

Her gaze narrowed and her face flushed with sudden color. Splaying her hands on her desktop, she leaned toward him. "You're having a temper tantrum because you lost, and you have the gall to accuse me of only wanting to win?"

"That's right, trying to win at any cost, and I emphasize the word 'trying.' " He leaned toward her, narrowing the distance, getting so close, he could see the faint freckles on her nose, smell her clean freshness. His teeth clenched as he reminded himself her character was neither clean nor fresh.

"You win the merger deal," he taunted, "but I can tell you one case you're going to lose, though it won't be from lack of trying, will it? I know all about Candy's history."

She pulled back, and he knew he'd struck home.

"So you end up being a party to a crime," he pressed on. "So what, as long as you win?"

"Get out of my office," she ordered, her eyes and voice glacial.

He stared at her for a moment, a deep sadness overwhelming him, replacing his anger. The realization hit him like a swift kick to the gut that he hadn't really believed the evidence until that moment, hadn't wanted to believe it. He'd expected her to deny it, tell him he was wrong. He turned away from her and strode out the door.

She slammed it behind him.

Bailey leaned against her door, trying to stop the trembling. She was angry, really angry. Through all their arguments, she'd never before felt like this, her stomach churning, her chest clenching, and, damn it, tears somehow finding their way out of her eyes. This was a fight, not an argument, not a contest. Austin had attacked her, and it hurt.

He must have won; she certainly hadn't.

She had expected he'd be a little upset about the merger, and she'd been prepared—not eager, but ready—to deal with that. But apparently he thought she'd known about Candy all along and was so immoral, she'd defend a criminal. "Win at any cost." Obviously he didn't have a very high opinion of her. She *wasn't* prepared to deal with that. She'd thought they were at least friends—well, friends with the added spice of sexual attraction thrown in. She'd begun to feel comfortable with him, close to him, especially after Saturday night. His words today were like a slap in the face. Obviously he didn't share her feelings.

She moved slowly back to her desk, to her work. She'd pull out a file and get busy, forget the cruel things Austin had said. After all, this wasn't the first time he'd won.

But it was the first time it mattered, the first time it hurt.

She snatched a tissue and blotted her eyes. If she didn't get those damned tears stopped soon, she'd be sobbing. She pressed the tissue hard against the corner of each eye, trying to push the treacherous moisture back inside.

The intercom on her phone buzzed. She took a deep breath and answered it.

"Come see me," Stafford snapped, then hung up.

Bailey slammed the receiver down, though it was too late for him to know it. Was there anybody else, she wondered, who would like to yell at her today?

She dug out the original sheet of yellow legal paper covered with names, case numbers, and other information she'd gathered at the courthouse. She was prepared for *this* confrontation.

She reached Stafford's office dry-eyed. After knocking twice, she entered without waiting for an invitation.

"Come in." He looked up as she flopped into a chair, but then he immediately returned to the paperwork on his desk. As though it were more important than she was, Bailey thought.

"You wanted to see me," she announced, ordering herself to control her temper. She wasn't a partner yet.

"That girl who's handling Miller . . ." He waved his arm in the air interrogatively.

"Margaret," Bailey supplied.

"Margaret brought me that file. Said you tried to get her to sign this 'Motion to Withdraw as Attorney of Record.' "

"How nice that she understood my request."

"You want to tell me why?" He flipped through the file.

"I told you why once. Now I have the proof." She tossed the paper onto his desk. To her dismay, it floated gracefully down. A sheet of paper didn't make a good throwing object.

"Hmmph. I can't read this. What is it? Shorthand?" He turned the notes back to her.

"No, it is not." Bailey at least had the pleasure of snatching it away from him. She read off the names, dates, and details of the previous, similar suit. "About the only difference, other than Candy's boyfriend's name, is that she was the one who ran into the boyfriend that time, and her insurance company was the one that got sued."

"And you think that proves, beyond a shadow of a doubt, that she's a fraud?" He rummaged in his desk drawer, came out with a cigar, and began rolling it between his fingers.

"It proves it to my satisfaction. Have you met the woman? She's horrible."

"Horrible people have a right to legal counsel, too." Bailey folded the sheet of paper and creased it firmly between two fingers. "Fine. We're not the only legal counsel in town. Let her go elsewhere."

"We agreed to take her case."

"Before we were aware of the facts." She folded the paper again.

"The facts being that she's been involved in a personal injury suit before, and she's horrible."

Bailey slammed her fist down on the desk. "What *is* the deal here? She's not one of our major clients. How did we get her in the first place? Is she somebody's sister? Is she sleeping with somebody important? We don't need her business, but we do need our good standing in the legal community."

Stafford nodded and turned his attention back to the file. "I'll go over it." He stuck the cigar in his mouth.

In disgust, Bailey turned to leave, but Morris' voice stopped her.

"Your notes."

"What for?" she demanded. "You can't read them."

He held out his hand and smiled. She passed him the multifolded paper and rushed out before she said something she'd probably regret. Probably, but not definitely.

"The man is a total, one hundred percent perfect jerk!" Bailey shouted as she pulled on her running shorts and dug her shoes out of the closet.

"Will you come in here so I don't have to yell?" Jodi called from the living room.

"Only if *I* can continue to yell." Bailey stomped across the room and flopped onto the floor in front of the sofa, where Jodi sat drinking a glass of Zinfandel wine.

"Can you sort of start at the beginning and tell me in chronological order exactly what happened?"

Bailey jerked her shoelace tight, then cursed when it

broke. "Austin's been trying to get our firm to merge with his."

"I know all that," Jodi interrupted. "Get on with the story between you and Austin."

"You know about the merger?" Bailey asked, pausing in her attempt to rejoin the pieces of her shoelace.

"You didn't think Stafford Morris typed up the merger documentation, did you?"

"Well, why didn't you say anything?"

Samantha leapt off the sofa and pranced over to crawl in Bailey's lap.

"Good grief, Bailey. You should know a legal secretary's job is confidential."

Bailey stroked Samantha's soft fur and cuddled her to her neck, feeling some loosening of the constriction in her chest. "Not confidential from somebody who already knows."

"You never brought up the subject. Have a glass of wine. You can't run with a broken shoelace." She shoved a full glass across the coffee table.

"I can run barefoot if I have to," Bailey declared, and Samantha squirmed at the angry tone. "Sorry, darling." She scratched a fuzzy ear, then slid the dog back to her lap while she resumed work on the shoelace. As dispassionately as possible, Bailey described Austin's violent entrance into her office.

"I just can't believe he would get so mad at you over a stupid merger," Jodi interrupted.

"Believe it. He did. He was vicious." Both shoes tied, Bailey set Samantha on the floor, put her feet together, and began to bounce her knees, stretching her thigh muscles.

"Did you try to explain your reasons?"

"Yes, I did. I told him I'd done what I considered the right thing, and then he accused me of representing Candy Miller even though she's a fraud, which is just what your boss is trying to make me do."

"So then did you tell him what you'd been doing about it?"

"Why should I? If that's what he thinks of me, I don't want anything to do with him." She stood and began more stretching.

"He'll get over it," Jodi encouraged.

"How nice for him. I won't."

She headed for the door. Behind her she heard Jodi say in a voice obviously meant to be overheard, "Samantha, I think your mommy's in love."

Bailey charged down the stairs and forced her legs to carry her across the parking lot, toward the street. Any minute now, she told herself, her muscles would become properly oxygenated, the adrenaline would start to flow, and she'd begin to enjoy this. The sun blazed heat down on her, and the concrete slammed it up into her face. Running in an oven took a lot of effort.

The run ranked right up there with her first venture out after a bout with pneumonia three years ago. Her legs felt like rubber bands, and each foot seemed to weigh twenty pounds. This business of fighting for real and dealing with scrunched-up insides apparently took a lot of energy. Not a pleasant thought.

Other thoughts dogged her, too, thoughts that involved running with Austin. And she had been, she realized, running *with* him. Until today, their competition had been a form of togetherness, a closeness. At least, it had been for her. Apparently the same wasn't true for the creep.

After only a mile, she headed back home in exhaustion.

"All right," she gasped, almost falling in the door, "I'm ready for wine now."

As she slumped on the sofa, Jodi shoved a glass in her hand. Samantha climbed to her shoulder and licked her sweaty face.

"To my friends," Bailey declared, laughing and raising her glass of wine. "Even though one of them has her head screwed on crooked." Bailey took a big gulp and was glad she had when Jodi spoke again.

"I've got it all figured out. By now Austin's probably feeling as rotten as you are, so you need to just pick up the phone and call him and explain."

Bailey pulled herself upright. "Is it your hearing or your comprehension that's defective? If I saw that man coming down the street, I'd go ten blocks out of my way to avoid him. Unless, of course, it had been raining and he was walking close to the street in a white linen suit and a car was headed for a huge puddle two feet away from him. Then I might stop to watch."

"Okay," Jodi agreed. "You're hurt. We'll leave it alone for right now."

"I am not hurt, but I would appreciate leaving it alone."

The three of them sat silently on the sofa while Bailey cast about for something to say. Her whole mind seemed to be filled with thoughts of Austin the Arrogant Creep. The only other thing she could dredge up was her visit to Stafford's office. And if she lost her partnership by losing her temper, she could lay that at Austin's door, too. Because of his tantrum, her temper had been a lot more volatile than normal.

But at least she'd come up with a new topic for discussion. "I suppose, since you seem to know everything else, that you've heard about the new partner," she ventured cautiously.

"I thought you'd never tell me!" Jodi exclaimed, smiling broadly and refilling both glasses. "Let's drink to that. Congratulations." She raised her glass in a toast.

Bailey grinned, a small ray of happiness shining through her gloom. "I wanted you to find out at the fiscal-year-end party. I wanted to march up there in some gorgeous dress I don't own yet and look back to see you watching. Gordon already knows, too. But you both have to promise to act surprised and excited!" She leaned back on the sofa and sipped her wine. "I don't know why they make such a big deal out of keeping everything secret."

Jodi shrugged. "It's like little kids when they have a club with lots of club secrets that aren't really secret and don't really matter anyway, but the kids get off on the secrecy idea."

Bailey burst into laughter. A good friend and a little wine after a run when one's heart was pumping furiously could affect marvelous mood changes, she decided. "You have a way of putting things into perspective. Stafford would be lost without you," she said.

"*I* know that, but *he* doesn't."

"Well, he will. I'll tell him. Just as soon as I'm officially a partner. You deserve recognition for your efforts." A sudden thought struck her. "Does Stafford pay you enough? I don't see you going on any spending sprees."

"Do they pay you 'enough'? Does anybody ever get paid 'enough'?"

"Sometimes." Bailey watched her friend's face closely.

Jodi refilled their glasses again and drained half of hers. "That may well be, but I doubt that any of those 'sometimes' ever happen in a legal secretary's life. And let me explain something else to you while we're on the subject of our different stations in life. In case it's escaped your attention after all these years, secretaries don't attend parties with attorneys."

Why was Jodi suddenly so defensive about her job? Bailey had never considered that they had "different stations in life."

"What are you saying?" she asked.

"Wake up, Bailey. Your little scenario where I get to see you made partner isn't going to happen."

Bailey set her wineglass on the table. Her mouth went suddenly dry. "You won't be there because you're a secretary? You also happen to be my best friend, and this will be my moment of glory. You and Gordon will both be there."

Jodi stood up. "I'm going to bed now. You'd better do the same and try to sober up."

Bailey didn't think she'd ever been more sober in her life.

"That just doesn't sound like Bailey," Gordon protested, signaling the bartender to bring them two more beers. "Her ethics are like everything else about her, black and white. Why, she jumped all over me one time because I pulled an uncanceled stamp off a letter."

"Evidently they shade into gray when it comes to winning," Austin said, dragging one finger through the condensed moisture on the outside of his beer mug. He'd felt a night on the town and a few drinks would be just the ticket to clear Bailey's treachery from his mind. However, the beer tasted as bitter as his thoughts, and he found he would prefer to be at home by himself, where he didn't have to make conversation.

Gordon shook his head. "No, I just don't buy it. You need to talk to her, give her a chance to explain."

Austin signaled for a fresh beer. Maybe this one would taste better.

He lifted it to his lips. It didn't. "Explain what?" he asked. "That she knocked my career in the head for the sake of winning, that she'll represent a client she knows is a fraud just so she doesn't have to admit defeat?"

Gordon laughed, an action Austin felt was totally inappropriate considering the seriousness of the situation. "Lighten up," Gordon said. "I seriously doubt that your career's ruined because you didn't get our firm. And I certainly don't think Bailey's so dumb or so spiteful as to base her career decisions on a chance to score a point in this endless contest you two have going." Gordon shifted on his stool to face the mirror behind the bar. "To tell you the truth," he continued, raising his beer in a salute to the reflections, "I'm glad it didn't go. I like things the way they are, and I sure don't want to have to work as hard as you do."

Austin scowled at the images in the mirror: one radiating sunshine even in the dark bar, and the other— himself—adding to the gloom. Okay, he had to admit, maybe Gordon was right. Probably he was right. Okay, so his friend was definitely right. So why did he still feel lousy?

He tilted his glass from side to side, watching the bubbles float around, examining the thoughts floating around in his mind. "I guess maybe it isn't the merger that's bothering me. That sort of lost its critical aspect when I found out the old grouch refused to hire me because of his own skewed perception of the ingredients for a successful firm, not because of my lack of qualifications. I guess the important issue here is Bailey's lack of morals in that asinine lawsuit."

Gordon nodded slowly. "Interesting," he said. "If this were just any lawyer we're talking about, you wouldn't be angry. You'd be excited about ripping their client to shreds, presenting your client with a real coup."

That was true, Austin had to admit. "But Bailey isn't 'just any lawyer.' She's—" He halted in midsentence, swallowed hard. *She's the woman I love*, he'd almost said. And even as he choked back the words, he knew they were true.

Good grief! What on earth did he do now? Setting aside the more obvious problems like their constant competition, how could he love an unethical attorney? His career, his life, were built on the preservation of justice and equity. How could he love someone who apparently didn't know the meaning of those terms? True, he admired her courage and her determination to win, but not when it meant dishonesty, a breach of ethics.

"She's what?" Gordon asked impatiently.

"Huh?"

"Bailey. You said she isn't just any lawyer. So what is she?" The smug look on Gordon's face suggested his friend had a good idea of the gist of his unfinished sentence.

But Austin was having enough trouble facing the knowledge himself; he wasn't ready to admit it to Gordon just yet. "She's pushy," he said. "Pushy, irritating, arrogant . . ." He hesitated again, at a temporary loss for adjectives. *Brilliant, exciting, sexy,* and *fun* were the only ones that came to mind.

"Yes?" Gordon prompted.

Austin sighed as images of Bailey danced through his head—Bailey's sweat-damp, exultant face after a run; Bailey expertly taking down the detective at the deposition; Bailey, sassy and sexy in that horrible wig at the bar; Bailey's ivory skin in the moonlight after they made love. Damn!

"She has the morals of a television evangelist," he growled, more to convince himself than Gordon.

Gordon shook his head. "You're wrong. I don't know what's going on, but I do know you're wrong. You've made a judgment based on circumstantial evidence."

Austin belted down half his beer in a sudden burst of anger, though he wasn't sure if the anger was directed at Bailey, Gordon, or himself. "After I left Stafford, I came right out and asked her about it, and all she did was order me out of her office. Slammed the door behind me. You don't consider that confirmation?"

Gordon laughed. "No, I don't consider that confirmation. I consider that anger and pride—qualities both of you seem to have an excess of. See that pay phone over there? Go call her and give her a chance to tell her side of the story. Isn't that what the law's all about? Innocent until proven guilty?"

Austin flinched at the way Gordon contrived to use his own ethics against him, and for a moment he considered taking his friend's advice. Gordon seemed so positive, and Austin wanted to believe him, wanted to believe in Bailey's innocence.

"She'd only hang up on me," he concluded. "She's already done that once, not to mention ordering me to leave her office and slamming the door behind me. I'll be damned if I'll give her the chance to do any of it again."

"Good boy," Gordon drawled. "Win at all costs."

THIRTEEN

"Bailey, old buddy! Hey, save that scowl for the clients. I'm on your side."

At Gordon's teasing words, Bailey made a conscious effort to rearrange her expression into something pleasant, something that didn't accord with the storm crashing around inside her head.

"You're certainly looking rested and complacent," she observed. "No more burning the eight-o'clock oil? Are we back to our former decadent life-style?"

Gordon slouched into one of her chairs. "We should all do what we do best. Anyway, Jodi likes me as a semi-lawyer."

Bailey leaned back in her chair and smiled. "Are we working up to a confession here?"

"Maybe. Have you got something of equal value to trade?"

"Hunh?"

"My confession for yours."

Sitting upright in her chair, Bailey folded her hands. "Then I guess we'll have to talk about the weather. My life is too dull to afford me any confessions."

Gordon laughed, unaffected by her aloof tone. Bailey

clenched her hands tighter. Sometimes, she thought, there could be such a thing as too much intimacy.

"Not even if we were to talk about a certain deceitful client and a certain pushy attorney from an opposing firm?" Gordon asked.

I'm not mad at Gordon, Bailey had to remind herself as her knuckles turned white. This is my friend, and he means well.

"Not even," she grated through clenched teeth, and was pleased as well as dismayed to see Gordon flinch slightly. While she hadn't meant to be rude to him, at least he realized she was serious. Surely he'd drop the subject now.

With a sigh he stood, closed the door, then returned to his seat. "I don't know what's going on, but I do know that my two best buddies are unhappy. To put it in language you can understand, don't you think it's time to schedule a conference and work out a settlement agreement?"

"If you weren't my friend, I'd tell you to mind your own business. Since you *are* my friend, I'll just say there are times when friends respect each other's privacy."

Gordon rose from the chair. "You got it," he said, and started for the door.

"Wait a minute," Bailey called. "We've dispensed with my confession, but what about yours? You were going to tell me about Jodi."

He paused with one hand on the door. "I could tell you friends respect each other's privacy."

Bailey slumped backward in her chair. "Oh, Gordon, I'm sorry. Please come back and sit down. I didn't mean to take out my anger on you."

"Are we going to talk about Austin now?" Gordon asked as he resumed his seat.

Bailey ignored his question. She didn't want to talk about or even think about Austin, though she wasn't having much success at the latter. "Did you know Jodi isn't coming to the year-end party?" she asked.

Gordon crossed his hands over his chest and looked smug. "Yes, she is."

"No, she's not. Secretaries *aren't allowed*. And Jodi's a secretary, making her, it appears, something less than a person according to the existing code."

"Not to worry. She's coming as my date, my fiancée."

Bailey's jaw dropped, came back up to form a smile, then a frown. "When did this happen? Jodi hasn't mentioned it. As of last night, she wasn't coming, and she certainly didn't say anything about marriage."

"I just figured it all out myself. I haven't told her yet."

"Don't you think it would be a good idea if you let her in on your plans?"

"I will at dinner on Saturday. Flowers, champagne, then a small black box. Maybe I'll even get down on my knees."

Bailey circled around her desk to hug him. "You really have turned into Prince Charming since Jodi showed up," she teased, settling into the chair next to his. She could have sworn he was blushing, though it was hard to tell beneath his tan.

He shrugged. "But on the practical side, I have to find out what size ring she wears. Any suggestions?"

"Sure. I can do that for you."

"I thought you might. I also thought you might go with me to pick out something she'd like."

"I'd love to. I'll even take off work on time."

"The ultimate sacrifice!" Gordon beamed as he stood to leave. "I'll hold you to it. My house at six tonight."

After Gordon left, Bailey sat staring out the window at the parking lot and office building next door, not really seeing either. Her lips curved up in a half smile. She couldn't think of anything that would please her more than the marriage of her two best friends. If she hadn't been so wrapped up in her own problems, she'd have seen it coming. In spite of Jodi's thorny shell, it was obvious she cared for Gordon. The fact that she continued to see him in spite of his occupation spoke volumes.

As for Gordon, in all the years they'd been friends, he'd never acted this way. Certainly there had been no lavender teddy bears or blushes!

Would anybody ever love her that way?

Bailey scowled at the last maverick thought and ordered it from her mind, but not before a recollection of the look of loathing on Austin's face as he left her office yesterday stabbed through her.

I'm happy. I'm happy for my friends, she told herself in an attempt to drive away the hollow, painful feeling that had suddenly returned.

This will at least solve the problems of Jodi's going to firm functions and of her low salary, Bailey reflected, diverting her thoughts to the positive side.

No, on closer examination, that wouldn't do. There was still the principle of the thing.

Somewhere around ten o'clock that morning Austin lost count of how many times he had picked up the phone with the intention of calling Bailey, then put it back down. By noon he estimated that the number exceeded a hundred.

Never had his emotions bounced around so wildly. After the initial shock had worn off, he'd begun to search for some explanation for Bailey's behavior. And against all the evidence, he'd come to believe, as Gordon did, that there must be some explanation—at least, he desperately *hoped* there was.

When and how had this irritating woman gained so much importance in his life?

He gulped down a dry sandwich and tried to return to his work. No one at the firm had been particularly upset or even surprised that the merger had failed. Some of the older partners gave him unsolicited but probably good advice on selecting a more likely firm next time.

Though he'd never admit it to anyone else, Austin acknowledged to himself that he'd pushed for the Hoskins, Grier firm as much from emotion as from factual data. His judgment had been influenced by his desire to change an old failure, an unaccustomed failure, to a success. Then, even when Morris' revelation had blunted the edges of the rejection, he'd pushed ahead with his plan because of Bailey. She became the one he wanted to conquer.

So how could he condemn Bailey for doing the same thing?

Except he hadn't done anything unethical in his effort to win, and she had—hadn't she?

He picked up the phone and, before he could change his mind, punched out her number.

Just hearing her voice identifying herself sent a rush of adrenaline through his body.

"Bailey," he began, talking fast before she could hang up on him, "I'm sorry I got upset about the merger. You had every right to vote the way you wanted. And if you'll just tell me why you're still representing Candy Miller, I'll try to understand."

She didn't hang up. To his surprise, her voice was calm, sweet even. "Understand? You think you can understand?"

"I think I can. Just try me." This was too easy.

"Blow it out your ear. Can you understand that?" She hung up.

An hour later a bomb came in the afternoon mail, a bomb in the form of a copy of the pleading he'd seen on Stafford Morris' desk. The smear of cigar ashes across the top had photocopied perfectly, identifying it beyond any reasonable doubt. He read it slowly, carefully, jubilantly. Hoskins, Grier and Morris was asking to be released as attorney of record for Candy Morris due to "pertinent facts of which said firm was not aware at the time of original filing."

This was the explanation he'd been looking for. Bailey had been trying to withdraw from the case, not pursue it. Her ethics were as beautiful as the rest of her. He clutched the piece of paper exultantly, barely able to restrain himself from tossing it into the air, from shouting to the heavens, from dashing out, grabbing the first person he saw, and forcing him to view this incredible document, prepared by the woman he loved.

He snatched up the phone, eager to share his joy with Bailey, then replaced it just as quickly. She'd only hang up on him again—and he couldn't blame her. As rude as he'd been, she'd probably never forgive him.

With a heavy sigh, he reached for the phone again. Might as well start crawling. Somehow, whatever it took, he had to make things right with Bailey.

Bailey's fingers drummed her desktop. She was still seething from Austin's condescending phone call at noon. Slamming the receiver in his ear had done little to decimate her anger. In fact, that latest addition had been like gasoline to the smoldering coals of her fire.

The more she thought about it, the hotter she became until flames finally erupted.

She shoved her chair back from her desk, crashing into the credenza behind her, and charged down the hallway to Stafford Morris' office.

Jodi looked up as she approached, then stood and reached for her arm, but Bailey was in no mood to be detained.

"What's wrong?" Jodi demanded.

Bailey shook off her hand and pushed into Stafford's office without even knocking.

"Come in, Bailey," he said, raising his eyes from the papers on his desk. "Have a seat. Make yourself comfortable."

Bailey tried to slam the door, but the obstinate thing closed slowly and quietly.

"I want to talk to you."

"By all means. Sit down."

"No!" She wanted to be able to tower over him. "I have three points to cover. Number one, representing that woman is wrong. I don't know why you're so insistent on doing it, but it's wrong. I refuse to be a party to it."

Stafford raised the hand clutching his cigar and started to open his mouth, but Bailey interrupted him.

"I'm not through. Number two, you treat Jodi despicably. She's my best friend. She's been there for all my important events, and she should be there to see me made partner. But that's really beside the point. Being a secretary doesn't make her another species. She's entitled to the same things we are. And that's not all," she declared as Stafford again started to speak. "Number three, this firm makes good money. We're not striving to make payroll, yet our accounting department tells me that our entire support staff is living barely above the poverty level. If you can't see the gross injustice of that, at least consider where you'd be without them."

The door flew open again, and Jodi burst into the room.

"Bailey, what on earth do you think you're doing?" she demanded, closing the door behind her and standing in front of it. "Please tell me this isn't because of what I said last night. I never intended—"

"I'm expressing my opinions, that's what I'm doing," Bailey interrupted. "Standing up for what's right. This is supposed to be an office of law, of justice and equity, and I haven't seen much of that lately."

"So you come in here and make a big scene. What's that supposed to accomplish?" Jodi made a move to take Bailey's arm.

Bailey sidestepped her. "At least I'm doing something. You hate this job, but you stay and take it."

"Until I get something better," Jodi agreed. "In the meantime, I start night school next month, so I don't need you taking me on as a cause."

"Something better?" Stafford roared. "You're planning to leave? You can't do that. I need you."

"She can, and she will," Bailey declared. "And I will, too, right now! You can take your stupid partnership and blow it out your ear. I don't care to be associated with partners who have no ethics!" She started for the door, motioning Jodi out of the way, then, on a sudden urge, turned back.

Stafford had just retrieved his cigar from the crystal ashtray and was moving it toward his mouth. Bailey snatched it from his grasp, crushed out the fire in the ashtray, then smashed the remaining three inches in the middle of Stafford's desk.

"Good-bye," she said, smiling and feeling satisfied for the first time in a while. "I'm going home."

"Take the rest of the day off, Bailey," he called after her, an act she felt somewhat diminished the impetus of her exit.

Sharon handed her a pink message slip as she dashed into her office to retrieve her handbag. Austin had called again. She crushed the paper into a tight ball and tossed it into her wastebasket.

That afternoon Bailey paced back and forth across the plush carpet of her living room, though its luxurious feel failed to imbue her with the usual sense of contentment and accomplishment. Her well-ordered life, her rising career, her comfortable home—everything was chaos now.

And the beginnings dated back to Austin's advent into her life. Somehow he was responsible for all her problems, even beyond those of which he was the direct and proximate cause. Like bringing sunshine and joy into her life, then replacing them with anger and sadness. She'd been perfectly content before he came along and taught her the thrill of besting him in a contest or even running a close second, not to mention the thrill of touching him, being held against his hard body. She hadn't had those things before he came along, and their absence hadn't seemed to leave a gaping hole inside her chest. But their removal sure did now, and that much was definitely his fault.

Everything else, she decided, from her problems with the Miller case to her fight with Morris, were indirectly Austin's fault.

She felt a soft touch on her ankle and looked down to see Samantha's bright eyes peering up at her.

"Oh, sweetheart!" Bending over, she scooped the fuzzy bundle into her arms and flopped onto the sofa. "As long as I have you, things aren't totally awful." Samantha planted a tiny lick on her chin, and Bailey smiled, cuddling the little animal.

The front door burst open, and Jodi called, "She's here."

"Who?" Bailey exclaimed, turning to see Jodi and Gordon coming inside.

"You," Gordon said, closing the door behind them. "Why didn't you answer the phone?"

Samantha leaped over the back of the sofa to greet the newcomers, and Bailey turned around to again face the window. "I couldn't think of anyone who might be on the other end that I wanted to talk to," she replied. That should give them a hint.

But it didn't. Jodi closed in on one side of her, and Gordon on the other.

"We've been worried about you," Jodi said.

Bailey stood and moved to a chair. "Obviously you wasted your concern. Why don't you two go to dinner or a movie or Las Vegas or something?" Surely they couldn't miss that hint.

"Bailey, I never intended to upset you so much last

night. Why didn't you say something to me before you attacked Stafford Morris with all guns blazing?'' Jodi asked.

Bailey reached down to where Samantha had curled at her feet and lifted the dog into her lap. Maybe if she ignored them, they'd go away and leave her to sort things out in private.

"Don't you think I'm capable of doing my own complaining?'' Jodi continued. ''Why did you risk your job over something that doesn't even affect you? You need to call Morris and apologize.''

"When rental rates on the Plaza go down,'' she grated.

"But you know it's not going to matter in the long run,'' Gordon interjected.

"Oh, sure,'' Bailey exclaimed, losing the few remnants of patience she'd had left. ''You'll marry Jodi, and she'll never have to worry about money again, but what about the person who takes her place? What about the other secretaries? What about the principle of the thing?''

"What makes you think he's marrying Jodi?'' Jodi interrupted, raising one eyebrow as she peered first at Bailey, then at Gordon.

"Way to go, friend,'' Gordon complained.

Bailey slumped lower in her chair and sighed. "Damn! I'm sorry, Gordon.''

Perched on the edge of the sofa cushion, Jodi somehow made a formidable appearance in spite of her diminutive size. ''Is this something the two of you have cooked up? Is this supposed to solve my problems? Marry Gordon and be an appendage? If that's not just like two lawyers!'' She sprang to her feet and started across the room, with Gordon right behind her.

Grabbing her shoulders, he turned her to face him. "Don't give Bailey so much credit,'' he said. ''It was my idea.''

Jodi turned her head to glare first at his right hand

on her shoulder, then at the left, then directly into his eyes. Gordon jerked his hands from her shoulders as though she had suddenly become a ball of fire.

"Can you help me out here?" he appealed to Bailey. "You got me into this."

"Don't give me too much credit," Bailey said with a laugh. "Anyway, I'd probably only make it worse. You're on your own, Romeo."

"Jodi, let's go to dinner and discuss this," he pleaded.

"No way. We're here to save Bailey from herself, and we can't leave until we do." She folded her arms and glared at him.

Gordon threw his hands up. "Fine. I wanted to do this right, with flowers and champagne and a diamond. Can you at least corroborate me on this, Bailey?"

"Absolutely. I'll give you a notarized statement. He asked me to help pick out a ring this evening, Jodi." Bailey stroked Samantha's head, enjoying the exchange, glad to be temporarily diverted from her own problems.

Jodi stood unmoving, making no response, but Bailey saw the corners of her mouth quiver slightly just before she compressed her lips to stop the incipient smile.

"Well?" Gordon demanded.

"Well what?"

"You're not going to make this easy, are you?"

"Why should I?"

Gordon rolled his eyes, then tried to take one of her hands. She tucked them neatly beneath her still-folded arms.

"I want to marry you," he shouted.

"So you two won't have your social consciences upset by watching me working for a creep, earning a pittance?"

"No. So I can live with you. So I can take care of you. Because I love you!"

Jodi's eyes wavered, and Bailey thought she was going to give up her resistance, but her stance didn't relax. "I don't intend to stop working at the firm until I get my degree."

"Your degree?" Gordon's eyes widened in surprise.

"She's going to night school," Bailey explained. "So she won't have to work for a creep and earn a pittance."

Gordon backed onto the sofa. "A legal secretary by day, a student by night—it doesn't sound like you've scheduled any time for me."

Jodi finally gave in and sat down beside him. "Maybe I could work you in on weekends and holidays."

Gordon shook his head. "Why couldn't I fall in love with a lazy woman?"

"I suppose for the same reason I couldn't fall in love with someone in an honorable profession."

As her two friends sat gazing into each other's eyes like total idiots, Bailey tried to tiptoe quietly from the room.

"Hold it!" Jodi called just before Bailey reached the safety of her bedroom door.

"I think the two of you can carry on from here without my help," Bailey protested.

"Maybe, but you haven't been carrying on very well without us."

"I'll try to do better in the future," she promised sarcastically, "if you'll just go away for a little while and let me have some time to sort out this mess."

Jodi nodded. "Will you promise to think about calling Stafford Morris to apologize? This is your career, Bailey. I know how important it is to you."

"True. But my career isn't dependent on Stafford Morris. I could open my own office." Though she hadn't considered it before, the idea didn't sound so bad. "And you could come to work for me."

"That's about as dumb as the time you decided to dye your hair black using fountain pen ink."

"Do I have any chance at all of getting rid of the two of you?" Bailey asked, ignoring Jodi's rude memory. There were obvious drawbacks to lifelong friends.

Finally, though, they left, arms wrapped around each other, sappy expressions on their faces.

But she and Samantha barely had time to get situated on the sofa before the doorbell rang.

Bailey studied the solid rectangle separating her from the outside world. She couldn't think of anybody she wanted to see. Moving Samantha to her shoulder, smiling as the little dog curled against her neck, she elected to ignore the doorbell.

The second ring was long and insistent and seemed louder, though of course, that was impossible.

Somehow she wasn't surprised to hear Austin's voice. "Bailey, I know you're in there, and I'm not going away until you open the door."

FOURTEEN

Austin knew he'd screwed up big time, but how could he apologize if Bailey wouldn't speak to him? He jabbed the doorbell again. When he'd passed Jodi and Gordon in the parking lot, they'd assured him she was home and even wished him luck, but they hadn't warned him he'd have to break down the door.

"I have something very important to tell you," he shouted.

"Go away before I call the police!"

That was progress. She was speaking to him now.

"Go ahead. I know a good lawyer." There was no sound of laughter from behind the closed door. "Bailey, I want to apologize. Please let me in."

"I can hear you just fine."

No doubt about it; she was definitely the most infuriating woman he'd ever met. If he could only figure out how to be happy without her in his life, he'd walk away. But he couldn't. "I was wrong," he said.

"Speak up. I can't hear you."

"I was wrong! I apologize. I should have never doubted you." If she ever forgave him, he'd strangle her for making him stand outside, shouting for all the world to hear.

The door remained closed.

"I got a copy of your motion to be released as Candy Miller's attorney of record. Bailey, I'm so sorry. I thought—"

The door burst open, cutting him off in midsentence, and she stood there with Samantha in the crook of one arm. His relief at seeing her, even though she was glowering at him, told him how anxious he'd been.

"Where did you get a copy of that motion?" she demanded.

"In the mail, from your office, of course." He reached inside his coat pocket, withdrew the paper, and unfolded it.

"Let me see that." She snatched it from him with her free hand, studied it a minute, then turned back in to her apartment, trying to push the door closed with one foot.

"Damn it!" Austin shoved his way inside. "It's bad enough you won't return my phone calls or answer the door, but stealing my document and closing the door in my face is going too far! I may be in love with you, but that doesn't mean I'm going to put up with your bad manners!"

She stalked across the room, set Samantha on the floor, and picked up the telephone. He was relieved to see that the number she punched in had too many digits to be 911.

Bailey listened impatiently to the sound of Stafford Morris' telephone ringing. He'd better be home, because she needed an answer now!

The ringing stopped and she heard Stafford's voice.

"I have here in my hand a copy of that blasted motion, *signed by you* as well as Margaret," she declared, dispensing with the formalities.

"Did you disturb me at home to tell me that? Obviously I already knew about it since I signed it."

"You said you weren't going to file it!" She waved the paper in the air as though he could see the gesture.

"No," he denied. "I just asked you why we should file it."

"And I told you why, as I recall." One foot began to tap the carpeted floor.

"You did. And a damn good job of it, too. We may put you into more courtroom work."

"Why didn't you tell me you'd filed it? You deliberately misled me."

"I tried to tell you, but you were too busy campaigning for the underdog and smashing my cigars."

Okay, she had to give him that point, but it only reminded her of the other reason she was angry at him. "So what are you going to do about the problems with the staff, now that we're on the subject?"

"If you stay around long enough to be an official partner and learn to talk below a roar, we might discuss what can be done."

"Well, yes, I can do that."

"Fine. Good-bye." He hung up.

Bailey cradled her own receiver. Stafford Morris still had a knack for taking the wind out of her sails. A little calmer, she turned back to face the storm in her living room.

Austin stood just inside the still open door, his expression intent and anxious. Waiting to see if she'd forgive him? Was it possible her forgiveness meant that much to him?

Then it hit her like a Kansas tornado. Somewhere amidst his ramblings, he'd said he loved her. For an instant her heart soared, the empty spot in her chest started to fill with a warm glow. Austin loved her. The halcyon days weren't over; they were just beginning. She took one eager step toward him, watched his lips relax into a smile and his arms come up to reach for her.

But reality intruded. He couldn't love her very much when he didn't trust her, had to have proof of her integrity. She halted in front of him. Wordlessly she proffered the wrinkled legal paper.

He returned it to his pocket, then reached for her. "Why don't we go out and grab a bite to eat?"

His arms pulling her close felt treacherously good. She slipped from his grasp while she still could. "Why don't we not?" she snapped, moving into a chair so he couldn't sit next to her, couldn't touch her.

He perched on the arm. "Bailey, I've apologized. There's nothing else I can do. I admit I was wrong. The whole damn world knows that by now."

"I accept your apology. But I see no point in further discussions. How can we be—" she hesitated "—friends if you don't trust me, if you have such a low opinion of me that you think—how did you phrase it? All that matters to me is winning. 'Right' isn't even a part of my vocabulary."

Though she wasn't looking at him, Bailey felt Austin flinch. "I'm sorry," he said quietly. "I was angry. That's not an excuse, just an explanation." He took her face between his hands, turned her toward him, forced her to look into his eyes. "If I didn't love you so damned much, you couldn't make me so damned angry, your conduct wouldn't be so important to me."

Bailey pushed his hands away and rose, moving about the room, avoiding him. How was she supposed to think coherently when he looked at her like that, his soul in his eyes?

"You certainly didn't waste any breath correcting my erroneous assumption," he called after her.

"I shouldn't have to," she retorted, looking around the room for Samantha. She could definitely use some of the little dog's unqualified love right now.

"No," he agreed, "you shouldn't have to. But it wouldn't have hurt if you'd tried. I'm only human. I have been known to be wrong upon occasion, especially when my emotions are involved. And they are very nvolved right now. Will you stop running around the oom and talk to me?"

He was wearing her down, getting to her, making er believe what she wanted to believe, what she was fraid to believe, setting her up for another letdown. 'It's been a long day. Can we discuss this another ime?" She peeked into the empty kitchen. "Samantha?" The dog didn't like it when people raised their oices, and was probably hiding somewhere.

"Fine," Austin said. "When?"

She had never met a pushier human being. "I don't know. Next week." Raising the sofa skirt, she peered underneath.

"What are you doing?" he asked.

"Nothing. Looking for Samantha. She has to be in ere. Both bedroom doors are closed." She checked behind the drapes.

"She wouldn't go outside, would she?" Austin asked, joining the search.

"She would if she could, but—the door! We left the door open!"

"She's probably around here somewhere," Austin soothed, and joined in the frantic search.

"I'm going to look for her outside," Bailey called, charging out the door.

"I'm coming with you," Austin responded, right behind her.

"You go that way," Bailey directed, flying off the last step. "Check all the bushes. She loves to smell. She'll sniff at one spot for ten minutes."

"We'll find her," Austin promised. "Traveling at that rate, she can't be far away."

In vain Bailey checked the dog's favorite spots—the patio where a Chow lived and both dogs issued bold threats as long as the fence stood between them; the garbage dumpster she always tried to steer Bailey toward; the tree used by the big dogs where she pawed the ground in her "macho" act.

Then, up ahead, she spotted a bit of black fur unde a bush. "Samantha!" she called. A black cat hissed a her and bolted away.

Behind the condo complex, she saw Austin ap proaching, empty-handed.

"She couldn't get past that." Bailey waved a hand a the stockade fence separating the condominium property from the housing subdivision behind. "She must be i front somewhere."

"She could be back at her own front door by now,' Austin soothed.

"Maybe." Bailey broke into a run, and Austin fol lowed suit.

Peering under cars, they searched the parking lot.

"I see her!" Austin called, and Bailey followed the direction his finger pointed.

In the middle of the busy four-lane street that passec in front of the complex, the little dog was inspecting turtle. "Samantha!" Bailey called, starting to run.

Samantha looked up for an instant, then returned to her interesting discovery, directly in the path of a large moving van just cresting the hill.

Bailey tried to run faster, pushed harder than eve before in her life, but she felt as if she were running through water. From the corner of her eye, she saw Austin stretching his long legs almost parallel to the ground with each step, but only the truck appeared to be moving rapidly.

Still several feet away, Bailey panicked as she real ized there was no way she could make it. At that same instant she heard the scream of brakes as Austin dove into the truck's path, and the truck, Austin, and Saman tha seemed to merge into one.

Hot wind pushed against her as the truck shrieked past. Her mind rejecting the horror, her momentum car ried her on, up to Austin's body lying curled beside the road.

"No!" she shrieked, stumbling over him into the ditch beside a still, furry ball.

For an instant she lay there, trying to summon the effort to get up, to face the probability that Austin and Samantha were both dead. Then she raised her head and found herself staring into a pair of bright brown eyes. Samantha licked her nose.

A surge of relief that her dog was safe mingled with fear for Austin. She snatched up Samantha and rushed to him.

Pressing her ear to his chest, she listened but wasn't sure if she heard Austin's heartbeat or only her own as it pounded more furiously than after the longest run. He couldn't be dead. She refused to even consider that idea. She loved him, and she wouldn't let him be dead.

Plopping Samantha down, she admonished her, "Stay!"

Trying desperately to fight back the panic and remember her long-ago instructions in CPR, Bailey pressed her lips to his and breathed in. "Don't you dare die!" she ordered, pushing on his chest. To her intense relief, a groan escaped, but his eyes remained closed, seemed to scrunch even tighter, as a matter of fact. Another good sign, she decided.

Bailey shook his shoulders frantically. "Get up and fight, damn you!" She bent forward to breathe into his mouth again and noticed his face was wet. For a moment she thought he was bleeding, then realized the moisture was clear and coming from her own eyes.

"Is he hurt?"

She looked up to see a tall, thin man approaching from the direction of the now stationary truck.

"Get an ambulance!" she ordered, and went back to her efforts.

"You jerk! I just go and fall in love with you and then you go and die!" She pressed her lips to his again, then straddled his supine body as the words of her CPR instructor came back through the panic. *If you don't hear cracking noises when you push on the rib cage you're not doing it hard enough. Better to have a broken rib than be dead.* She pushed with all her might.

Austin cursed.

He was alive! She gave another push since the last one had been so successful.

He cursed again, roundly and loudly. Yes, he was definitely alive.

"Are you trying to kill me? Didn't they teach you the difference between CPR and breaking a man's ribs?"

Laughing and crying, Bailey fell onto his chest, holding him close. "I thought you were dead!"

He wrapped his arms around her. "Had you worried, huh?"

She snuggled against his neck. "Yes, you had me worried."

"Did you mean what you said?"

"Huh?"

"About being in love with me."

Bailey raised her head and gaped at him. "You were unconscious! You couldn't have heard that!"

"Did you mean it?" He grinned.

"You weren't unconscious at all, were you?"

"Well, that truck did knock the wind out of me. Then you gave such nice mouth-to-mouth, I just didn't see any reason to get up until you started trying to break my ribs."

Bailey jumped to her feet. "You creep! You arrogant jerk! You had me all upset and worried, and you let me make a total fool out of myself saving your life when you didn't need saving!" She bent to scoop up Samantha, then glared back down at Austin. He was still smiling, totally unrepentant.

"Come back here and finish saving my life," he said. "And don't pull that anger business on me. I've got your number now, Bailey Russell. I've seen you when you're really mad." He raised his arms invitingly.

He was right. She wasn't really upset with him, but she wasn't going to give in so easily. "You don't look very dignified lying in that ditch. I will not get down there with you. Get up and come on back to my place. As I recall, we were discussing the error of your ways before this interruption."

He groaned in mock agony and started to rise, then groaned more loudly, more sincerely, and fell back.

"Forget it," Bailey said, trying to suppress a smile. "No more mouth-to-mouth in the ditch."

But when he looked up at her, his face had lost its smile, and beads of perspiration stood out on his forehead. "I think I twisted something in my right leg," he said, his matter-of-fact tone belying the pain in his eyes.

"Take my hand," Bailey offered, suddenly alarmed that he had a real problem.

He shook his head. "I'm all right. Just give me a minute." Again he tried to rise, made a grotesque face, and sank back down.

Bailey stooped beside him and tentatively examined his leg, eliciting a loud curse from him.

"It's a damn good thing you decided to practice law and not medicine," he complained. "Are you still trying to kill me?"

"I think your ankle's sprained," Bailey told him.

"And just what do you base this diagnosis on, Dr. Russell?"

"The fact that I don't recall your ankle being the same size as your thigh prior to the present time," she snapped.

Austin moaned as he raised his head and twisted around in an attempt to view the limb under discussion.

"Don't worry," she reassured him. "The man in the truck went to call an ambulance."

"I'm not going to lie here in this ditch and wait for an ambulance." He tried again to get up, this time making it to a posture somewhere between sitting and stooping.

"I think you injured your brain as well as your leg. Get back down before you do more harm."

As he began to totter, Bailey rushed over and grabbed his arm. This time he didn't protest. Returning Samantha to the ground, she helped him stand, one arm draped around her neck, his injured leg dragging. Extending her free hand to Samantha, she caught the dog as she jumped, cradling her in the crook of her arm.

"Okay, Mr. Macho. What now?"

"Your place," he whispered, taking in deep gulps of air.

The truck driver rushed up. "Mister, you ran right out in front of me. It wasn't my fault."

Austin waved him away.

"I called an ambulance," the man said, hovering over them as they started across the street. "It's on the way."

"Uncall it," Austin ordered.

"Send it across the street," Bailey said, countermanding the order as they continued on their way. "Number 219. Or the stairs leading up to 219. You'll never make it up those steps."

"I can make it up your stairs with no problem."

"Maybe with my help."

They moved in silence for a few seconds with Austin hopping on his good leg, leaning heavily on her.

"We make a pretty decent team," he ventured as they left the pavement for the driveway.

"Stands to reason," Bailey agreed. "When you have the best and the second best on the same team . . ." She grinned up at him tauntingly.

In an unexpected movement, he pulled her to him for a quick kiss, almost upsetting their unstable balance.

"You never did answer my question about whether you meant what you said when you were mauling me," he pointed out as they teetered in the middle of the parking lot.

"I don't say things I don't mean." She hesitated for a moment, then asked shyly, "Did you mean what you said?"

"*I'll* even repeat what I said," Austin replied. "I love you, Bailey Russell. And I'd like to propose a merger, make our team official."

"A merger? You want to start our own law firm? No, I don't think so. I could never work with you. You're too pushy."

Austin threw back his head and laughed, then urged her on to continue their slow trek. "*I'm* pushy? *You're* the pushiest person I've ever met. But one day, yes, I do want us to have our own firm. We'll be unbeatable. However, right now I'm just asking you to marry me."

He tossed out the words so casually, it took a minute for their meaning to sink in. When it did, her heart rate accelerated, and her blood rushed to and fro ecstatically.

Marry Austin. Roll over in the middle of the night and find him there beside her. Raise children with his incredible eyes who'd be able to run faster than both their parents.

"People who're in love do it a lot, you know," Austin said when she didn't reply. Then, more seriously, "I won't go so far as to say I'd die without you, but the outlook would be pretty bleak. I want to spend the rest of my life with you, loving you, fighting with you—"

"Not fighting," she interrupted with a shudder. "Competing, maybe, but I don't ever want to fight with you again. That was awful."

They reached the stairs to her apartment and sank down on the bottom step. With a groan, Austin stretched his injured leg out in front of him.

"I'm sorry, sweetheart," he said, his fingers touching her cheek gently. "I promise never to mistrust you again." He cleared his throat. "So what do you say? Are we going to make it legal?"

Samantha chose that moment to squirm from Bailey's armlock and into Austin's lap, rolling over to allow him to rub her stomach.

"There are still a few issues to be negotiated," Bailey said mischievously. "You have to adopt Samantha."

Austin rolled his eyes. "Okay, I'll adopt Samantha. What else?"

"I'm not going to cook."

"Thank goodness," Austin mumbled.

"What?"

"I said, that's fine."

"Okay, then," she agreed casually.

" 'Okay'? I offer you my heart, my soul, my name, even agree to adopt your dog, and all you say is 'okay'?" he exclaimed in mock consternation.

She laughed and leaned against him, wrapping her arms confidently around him. "Yes, Austin Travers," she whispered. "I love you. I want to marry you."

"That's a little better," he said, grinning, as he pulled her to him.

"Race you down the aisle," she said just before his lips claimed hers.

SHARE THE FUN . . .
SHARE YOUR NEW-FOUND TREASURE!!

You don't want to let your new books out of your sight?
That's okay. Your friends can get their own. Order below.

No. 148 ANYTHING YOU CAN DO by Sara Garrett
The more Bailey fought Austin, the more he wanted to win her heart.

No. 32 SWEET LAND OF LIBERTY by Ellen Kelly
Brock has a secret and Liberty's freedom could be in serious jeopardy!

No. 33 A TOUCH OF LOVE by Patricia Hagan
Kelly seeks peace and quiet and finds paradise in Mike's arms.

No. 34 NO EASY TASK by Chloe Summers
Hunter is wary when Doone delivers a package that will change his life.

No. 35 DIAMOND ON ICE by Lacey Dancer
Diana could melt even the coldest of hearts. Jason hasn't a chance.

No. 36 DADDY'S GIRL by Janice Kaiser
Slade wants more than Andrea is willing to give. Who wins?

No. 37 ROSES by Caitlin Randall
It's an inside job & K.C. helps Brett find more than the thief!

No. 38 HEARTS COLLIDE by Ann Patrick
Matthew finds big trouble and it's spelled P-a-u-l-a.

No. 40 CATCH A RISING STAR by Laura Phillips
Justin is seeking fame; Beth helps him find something more important.

No. 41 SPIDER'S WEB by Allie Jordan
Silvia's quiet life explodes when Fletcher shows up on her doorstep.

No. 43 DUET by Patricia Collinge
Adam & Marina fit together like two perfect parts of a puzzle!

No. 44 DEADLY COINCIDENCE by Denise Richards
J.D.'s instincts tell him he's not wrong; Laurie's heart says trust him.

No. 46 ONE ON ONE by JoAnn Barbour
Vincent's no saint but Loie's attracted to the devil in him anyway.

No. 47 STERLING'S REASONS by Joey Light
Joe is running from his conscience; Sterling helps him find peace.

No. 48 SNOW SOUNDS by Heather Williams
In the quiet of the mountain, Tanner and Melaine find each other again.

No. 51 RISKY BUSINESS by Jane Kidwell
Blair goes undercover but finds more than she bargained for with Logan.

No. 54 DAYDREAMS by Marina Palmieri
Kathy's life is far from a fairy tale. Is Jake her Prince Charming?

No. 55 A FOREVER MAN by Sally Falcon
Max is trouble and Sandi wants no part of him. She *must* resist!

No. 56 A QUESTION OF VIRTUE by Carolyn Davidson
Neither Sara nor Cal can ignore their almost magical attraction.

No. 57 BACK IN HIS ARMS by Becky Barker
Fate takes over when Tara shows up on Rand's doorstep again.

No. 59 13 DAYS OF LUCK by Lacey Dancer
Author Pippa Weldon finds her real-life hero in Joshua Luck.

No. 60 SARA'S ANGEL by Sharon Sala
Sara *must* get to Hawk. He's the only one who can help.

No. 61 HOME FIELD ADVANTAGE by Janice Bartlett
Marian shows John there is more to life than just professional sports.

No. 62 FOR SERVICES RENDERED by Ann Patrick
Nick's life is in perfect order until he meets Claire!
